NEWARK PUBLIC LIBRARY-NEWARK, OHIO 43055
3 2487 00729 5190

Strange Company

Also by Robert J. Conley in Large Print:

Fugitive's Trail
A Cold Hard Trail
Wilder & Wilder

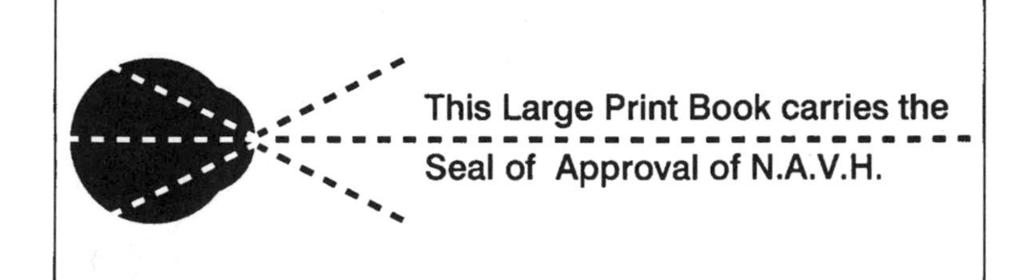

Strange Company

Robert J. Conley

Thorndike Press • Waterville, Maine

This book is a work of fiction. Names, characters, places and incidents are either the product of the author's imagination or are used fictitiously. Any resemblance to actual events or locales or persons, living or dead, is entirely coincidental.

Published in 2002 by arrangement with
Cherry Weiner Literary Agency.

Thorndike Press Large Print Western Series.

The text of this Large Print edition is unabridged.
Other aspects of the book may vary from the original edition.

Set in 16 pt. Plantin by Myrna S. Raven.

Printed in the United States on permanent paper.

Library of Congress Cataloging-in-Publication Data

Conley, Robert J.
Strange company / Robert J. Conley.
p. cm.
ISBN 0-7862-4302-3 (lg. print : hc : alk. paper)
1. United States — History — Civil War, 1861–1865 — Fiction. 2. Racially mixed people — Fiction. 3. Cherokee Indians — Fiction. 4. Prisoners of war — Fiction. 5. Male friendship — Fiction. 6. Large type books. I. Title.
PS3553.O494 S76 2002
813′.54—dc21 2002068703

For my friend
and teacher,
Bob L. Neal

Author's Note

Although *Strange Company* is fiction, the Battle of Pea Ridge, or the Battle of Elkhorn Tavern, was only too real for the 1,203 men who died there. Where details of the battle are used in the first two chapters, I have tried to keep them historically accurate, or nearly so. I have also used real names of historical figures who participated in the battle. My information on the Battle of Pea Ridge came primarily from four sources: *General Stand Watie's Confederate Indians* by Frank Cunningham (Naylor, 1959); *The Battle of Pea Ridge, 1862,* a pamphlet of "Material Reviewed by Superintendent Pea Ridge National Park Printed by Shofner's, Rogers, Arkansas" and available at the Park; *Blue & Gray Magazine*, Volume V, Issue 3, January 1988, a special issue on the Battle of Pea Ridge; and a tour of the battlefield itself and of the facilities and displays provided by the National Park Service.

Scholars, if they read this book, might take exception with me on two points, so I will explain myself here and then let it go. There is debate on whether or not the description of Pike's appearance at Pea Ridge as given by his biographer Fred W. Allsopp is accurate. I have chosen to make use of Allsopp's description as being the most dramatic and therefore the most useful for my purposes as a novelist. Also, Dhu Walker's translation of the place name, Tahlequah, is not the commonly accepted translation. It is a translation that I heard from a native speaker of Cherokee who maintains firmly that it was the original meaning and that usage has changed it over the years.

Robert J. Conley
Tahlequah, Oklahoma
August 1990

1

Pike was a flamboyant son of a bitch. Everyone knew that. But this time he had outdone himself. His command was made up of three regiments of Choctaws, Chickasaws, Cherokees, Creeks, and Seminoles from the Indian Territory. Among these Indians there were occasional hints of tribal clothing — a feather in a hat, a cloth turban, a bright red sash across the breast, a finger-woven yarn belt, or a beaded belt. A few wore Confederate army uniforms or pieces of uniforms, but most dressed like white southern frontiersmen, some in buckskins, others in homespun cloth. A significant number of the soldiers were of mixed blood and looked more white than Indian.

Nevertheless, Albert Sidney Pike — Bostonian turned southerner, Harvard man, poet, translator, lawyer, Freemason, and brigadier general in the Army of the Confederate States of America — had a fanciful imagination with a romantic twist. His three regiments were Indian, and he chose to drape his three-hundred-pound bulk appropriately. He wore soft buckskin leggings with horizontal stripes of vermilion around the calves and thighs and a vertical stripe down the outside of each leg made of porcupine quills dyed red, yellow, and green. He was shod in soft moccasins finely decorated with colorful glass trade beads. His expansive chest and belly were covered by a buckskin tunic that matched the leggings in material and decoration. The tunic, with its long fringe, hung clear to his knees, and the sleeves were also fringed. In addition, each sleeve had a stripe of colored quillwork on the outside just like the one on the legging below it. A circular design of the same colored quills covered each of Pike's breasts, and he wore a massive necklace of bear claws, which was mostly hidden by his long, full gray beard. Curly gray hair lay on his shoulders and cascaded down his back. All of this was topped off by a full eagle-feather headdress.

No one bothered to tell Pike that his outlandish northern plains-style costume was as foreign and exotic to his Indian charges as it was to Pike himself. Had anyone bothered, it is likely that Pike would not have listened. He was a strong-headed man, even when he was wrong-headed. And as if the general did not cut a ludicrous enough figure alone, he had chosen to coerce John Ross, the principal chief of the Cherokee Nation, to ride alongside him in a buggy. The Indian chief, who was seven-eighths Scottish, wore a black cutaway coat and matching trousers with a vest, a white shirt, and a nattily knotted black silk tie. Ross wore shiny black high-button shoes and spats, and atop his neatly trimmed short reddish hair sat a black stovepipe hat. He carried a stylish walking stick. The buggy in which this mismatched pair rode was driven by Brutus, the general's black body servant, who also carried papers and payrolls in garish carpetbags.

Riding along pompously at the head of his army, Pike was like a grand tragedian on the stage, although his audience was behind him. He had forgotten his earlier anger at the orders that would send him to lead his Indians — he always called them that — into battle in Arkansas. The strategy was not only ill advised, he had told General Van Dorn, but illegal as well, since the Confederacy's treaties with the tribes had promised to use the Indian troops exclusively in Indian Territory.

"My Indians," Pike had roared, "are poorly suited for use in full-scale battle.

They are much better adapted to hit-and-run tactics."

But the orders were not rescinded. The entire state of Missouri was to be the prize, and Pike reluctantly obeyed. Now he rode forth with a smug arrogance born of overweening pride and sustained by a colossal, innate dramatic flair.

Right behind the buggy, at the head of the Cherokee mixed-blood contingent, rode Colonel Stand Watie and his nephew, Elias C. Boudinot. Colonel Watie, a full-blood Cherokee known as a progressive, was the leader of a large faction of mixed-blood tribal members. He had declared himself principal chief of the Confederate Cherokee Nation, and his relentless attacks on Tahlequah, the capital city of the Cherokee Nation, had finally forced John Ross, a staunch believer in neutrality, to accept a treaty with the Confederacy. General Ben McCulloch, famous former Texas Ranger, and his Texas Battalion rode with Watie and his breeds.

Colonel John Drew came next with some Cherokees known as Pins. They were mostly on foot, eating the dust of Pike's buggy and Watie's and McCulloch's mounted cavalries. Though the Cherokee Nation had remained neutral up until the forced treaty with the Confederacy, groups of Union-sympathizing Cherokees had been organized to combat Watie's Confederates, largely because of the powerful influence of the abolitionist Baptist missionary John Jones and his son, Evan. These largely traditional Pin Indians, most of whom were full-blood Cherokees, got their name from a secret identifying pin worn under their coat lapels. When their chief, John Ross, signed the Confederate treaty, they found themselves suddenly inducted into the ranks of their enemy.

Roderick Dhu Walker, half Cherokee, trudged along on foot in the midst of the Pins. Dhu would have looked more in place among Stand Watie's mixed-bloods, but his sympathies were with the more traditional full-bloods. Dhu had no uniform. He wore store-bought trousers tucked into almost knee-high black boots, a muslin shirt, and a dark jacket, and underneath the lapel of the jacket he wore his pin. Dhu's hair was dark brown, not quite black, and cropped neatly just short of shoulder length. He wore in his belt a long hunting knife and carried an old shotgun. Dhu longed for a horse. He was a pretty good horseman, and his family had owned three fine horses before the war. The war in its early stages had cost Dhu everything. His family had all been killed, the house burned to the ground, and the horses stolen by Stand Watie's soldiers. Dhu figured his three horses were probably up there underneath three of Watie's mixed-blood gray suits. He was filled with resentment and confusion. His sympathies were not with the South; it was the southern states that had driven the Cherokees out of their homelands and into the West. He had no use for the southern states or for southern whites, and yet here he was marching into battle as a Confederate soldier. And the chief to whom he was loyal, John Ross, Cooweescoowee, rode up ahead in a carriage with the ludicrous Pike. Dhu wondered if Ross was confused and bitter, too. He probably was. Ross had not wanted this shift in allegiance to the Confederacy. Everyone knew that. He had practically begged the United States to send troops into the Cherokee Nation to protect its neutrality as they were obligated to do by treaty. But the Union had not granted his requests and the Confederate troops had ridden right into Tahlequah and forced John Ross to sign the sham treaty. So here they were, marching into battle to kill Yankees.

Dhu did not think he could kill a Yankee. Why should he? He wondered what he would do in the heat of battle. He wondered what the other Pins would do. He was certain they all felt the same way he did about the mess they were in. Dhu Walker was confused, but his confusion was not a result of ignorance or stupidity. He was a graduate of the Cherokee Male Seminary and of Saint Louis University. He was well schooled in the classics and could speak, read, and write English, Cherokee, Greek, and Latin. He had taught for a couple of years in the Cherokee Nation's free compulsory public school system. Then he had decided that teaching was not the life for him, and he had resigned and returned home to help his father raise horses. The war had put an end to all of that. The schools were closed. His home was gone. Dhu was bitter toward the United States for having allowed the Cherokee Nation to be victimized by the southern states. He was bitter toward the mixed-blood southern sympathizers, and he was filled with hatred for the nameless, faceless men who undoubtedly rode his horses somewhere up ahead in the long column that was winding its way toward Pea Ridge.

"Inoli."

Someone had called Dhu by his Cherokee name, Badger. He looked up. Yona Galegi, Climbing Bear, had dropped back to walk beside him.

"Inoli," Yona said, "what are you going to do?" He spoke in Cherokee.

"What do you mean?" Dhu said, also using his native tongue.

"When we get in the big fight, what will you do?"

"I don't know," Dhu said. "We're walking with our enemy. We're on the wrong side."

"We have been talking up there ahead," said Yona. "Maybe the talk came from John Drew. I don't know. We've agreed that we will not kill Yankees."

Dhu was silent for a few paces.

"Will you kill Yankees?" Yona asked.

"No, I won't kill Yankees. Maybe I'll kill southerners."

"Yes," Yona said. "That would be a good surprise for them."

Dhu glanced back over his shoulder. The long line of Indian soldiers seemed from his point of view to have no end. Colonel Cooper came behind the Pins with his Choctaw and Chickasaw units. Led by their bearded commander, a white man, the Choctaws and Chickasaws were as ragtag a bunch as the Cherokees. A mixture of full-bloods and mixed-bloods, they were poorly dressed and poorly armed. The Seminoles were next, led by their Confederate chief, John Jumper, who was a major in the Confederate army and an ordained Baptist preacher. Last in line — some mounted, some on foot — were the Creeks under Colonel Daniel McIntosh, himself a mixed-blood Creek. He had given commissions to eight of his relatives, and they all rode with heads held high and long hair flying in the breeze. Many of their followers, however, walked.

The Indian soldiers who walked and rode toward Pea Ridge that day knew vaguely that their task was to drive the federal forces out of Missouri. They did not know the significance of that mission. They did not know the importance of controlling Saint Louis. They did not know that Brigadier General Samuel R. Curtis, federal commander of the Southwestern District of Missouri, had left Rolla, Missouri, along the old Telegraph Road headed for Arkansas, and on the way had captured and occupied Springfield without a fight. The Confederates had been pushed out of Missouri, but they had not given up on Missouri. They had retreated into Arkansas to regroup, and they were being pursued by the forces of General Curtis. The Indian soldiers did not know all these details, but they had heard vague talk that the reason they were being marched out of Indian Territory into Arkansas was to join forces with other Confederate troops in a major effort to drive the federal forces back out of Arkansas.

Stand Watie and his ilk were enthusiastic about this chore, but it had been a long march into the Ozark Mountains of Arkansas from the foothills in Indian Territory. Even the horsemen were weary. The foot soldiers were sore and exhausted. But alone in the midst of this bizarre army, in addition to the general physical misery they shared with the rest, the Pins smoldered with resentment and animosity. Convinced that they had been abysmally betrayed, they moved sullenly forward, harboring a secret but dogged determination to fail.

2

By nine o'clock on the morning of March 7, 1862, the Indians knew that the battle had begun. They were camped eight miles northeast of Bentonville, Arkansas. They could hear the shots, but apparently Pike had not yet received his orders. The Indians milled around the camp, many of them frustrated and eager to see some action. Dhu Walker was not one of those; he was not looking forward to the battle. A little at a time, Dhu heard rumors about what was taking place up ahead. Curtis, the Union commander, believed that the Confederates would attack from the south by way of Telegraph Road. At a place where Telegraph Road crossed Little Sugar Creek, Curtis had placed a heavy concentration of soldiers, and he had ordered trees cut down to block the road. To the north of the blocked road and the creek stood some high bluffs. On these, the general had placed troops and cannons.

Then Dhu heard that Confederate General Van Dorn had planned simultaneous attacks on both Union flanks. The force to the Union's left would also attack from the rear.

"We're whipping the Yankees on the left flank," he heard someone say.

At last Pike's orders arrived, and the Indians, along with the Texans, began to move. Again they marched, they knew not where. They moved along the Bentonville Detour west of Pea Ridge Mountain. They passed through the tiny village of Leetown. North of Leetown, the thick woods on either side of the road suddenly gave way to a large open prairie. The federals saw them first, but only by a few seconds. As the federal cannons roared, the rebels ran to the sides of the road. Ben McCulloch ordered a charge, and the Confederate soldiers began the attack in two groups, issuing loud rebel yells. Across the field, Union troops refused to obey an order to counterattack.

Stand Watie's mixed-bloods led the assault on the three federal cannons. The Pins lagged behind. After a brief but violent struggle, a Yankee shouted "Turn back," and the defenders turned and ran. The Confederate Indians pranced around the three captured cannons, whooping and cheering, congratulating themselves. Dhu was hanging well back, but he thought that he had seen Yona stab one of Watie's men from behind. Then Dhu heard Stand Watie order the Yankee gun carriages burned, and soon flames were crackling around the cannons. Then there was a tremendous explosion, and Dhu heard screams. He was not close enough to see well, but he thought several Indians had been hurt, possibly killed. There must have been some powder in the cannon tubes, he thought. Fools, for standing so close to the flames.

Then there was another more distant roar, and another. A cannonball hit in their midst. Then a second hit and bounced. The Indians ran, not waiting for orders, not asking permission. Another federal gun emplacement across the field was firing at them. In the shouting and confusion, Dhu, along with many others, found refuge in the woods. The trees were thick, and it was cool and dark in there. He felt a little safer. He had gotten through the first skirmish without having to kill.

He wandered deeper into the woods, no longer interested in how the battle was going. He would just try to stay out of sight and find his way home. This was a white man's war anyway. Then the Texan was there in front of him, holding a .44 caliber Remington percussion revolver in his right hand. The two men startled each other at first; then the Texan recovered.

"You're going the wrong way, soldier," he said. "Turn around."

Dhu raised his shotgun and fired, and the Texan fell backward, his chest a bloody mess. Dhu picked up the Remington and stuck it in his waistband. He reloaded the shotgun with a shell from his coat pocket and continued on his way.

While the battle raged near Leetown, a second battle was being fought at Elkhorn Tavern, a waystation on Telegraph Road, at the opposite end of the Union lines. This was where the federals had expected the Confederate charge to come up Telegraph Road. Instead, the rebels had circled around and come up behind the Yankees. Private Benjamin Franklin Lacey, First Iowa Battery, was helping man the guns in Clemens' Field, east of the tavern, when the order came to face about. Lacey was helping to turn the big cannon when a Confederate shell struck an ammunition caisson not far away, causing a tremendous explosion and costing the federals a significant quantity of their ammunition. Lacey threw himself to the ground and covered his head. Then he heard shouting.

"Come on! Come on! Get the lead out!"

He scrambled to his feet. The other gun crew, not so close to the explosion, already had its gun turned. Lacey grabbed the carriage and heaved. Soon the gun was turned to face the attacking rebels. Lacey spiked the ring to help stabilize the big gun, while the fourteen-year-old powder monkey ran around to the front end with a bag of powder. The loader rammed it home, and then another Confederate explosive shell hit yet another caisson. The gun crew all fell on their faces and covered their heads. They were back on their feet and ready to fire when they heard the order.

"Fall back! Fall back!"

Lacey pulled up the spike and the six-man crew began dragging the cannon backward. Suddenly rebel yells were all around. Gray-suited cavalrymen thundered by and circled around, swinging their shining sabers. Lacey saw the powder monkey fall, a rifle ball between his eyes. Then he felt a powerful impact from behind as a cavalryman rode straight into him, and he felt a dull thud on the back of his head, and his world went black.

The day ended with Dhu still hiding in the woods. As the sun went down, the firing ceased. Dhu had no idea who had won the day or even if the battle was over. He found some hardtack in his coat pocket. It wasn't much, but he was hungry. He ate it and longed for a drink of water. The more he thought of it, the thirstier he became. He knew the countryside was full of creeks and streams. He had crossed enough of them in the last two days. It shouldn't be hard to find one. He stood up and started to wander in the dark. He had no idea where he was going, no idea what direction he was traveling. But he thought that if he wandered around long enough, he was bound to locate some water. Even if he couldn't see, he would be able to hear the water run. He wandered on, stumbling in the dark. The canopy of leaves overhead shut out even the meager light from the stars and the moon. He fell and bruised the heel of his hand on a rock. He got up to his hands and knees, still clutching the shotgun, breathing deeply and listening; he heard the rippling of a small mountain spring. He stood up and moved toward the welcome sound. In six steps he was there, and he dropped again to his knees. Laying the shotgun aside, he stretched out on his belly and lowered his face into the cold, fresh water. He drank his fill, but the gnawing hunger had returned to his belly. He had no more biscuits. He felt the ground alongside the water and discovered that the stream, which was narrow enough to step across, flowed right out of a hillside. He sat down beside the source, leaned back in the grass, and slept.

He awoke to the sound of gunfire. So the battle was not over. The generals had merely decided to let the soldiers get a good night's sleep before continuing to kill and die. He stood up and stretched, then picked up his shotgun and started walking again, away from the sound of the guns.

When Benjamin Franklin Lacey came to his senses and tried to get up, he discovered that his hands were tied securely behind his back. He wriggled around and sat up, and the motion made his head hurt. He groaned.

"Well, Yank," he heard someone say in an accent that was strange to his ears, "so you ain't dead after all."

He looked up. Standing not six feet away was another private about his age, but this one wore gray.

"No," Lacey said. "I can tell I ain't dead 'cause I hurt too bad."

"Tell you the truth," said the rebel, "I'm glad. You're the first prisoner I've ever been give the guard of. I'd hate for you to've turned out dead. Where you from, Yank?"

"Iowa," Lacey said. "Right now I wish I'd never left. What about you?"

"I'm from Louisiana. Come up with Major Hebert. Name's Johnny Comeaux. What's yours?"

"Benjamin Franklin Lacey," said Lacey, suddenly stiffening. This friendly chat somehow didn't seem appropriate under the circumstances. He was, after all, Comeaux's prisoner. But he reconsidered quickly. An unfriendly guard would be much worse. "They call me Ben."

"You want a drink of water, Ben?" said Comeaux.

"Yeah."

Comeaux reached into a water barrel with a dipper, then slung his rifle over his shoulder and took Ben by the arm.

"Let me give you a hand up," he said. "I ain't allowed to untie you, so I'll have to hold the dipper."

He pulled Ben to his feet and held the dipper while Ben gulped water. Finished, Ben gasped for breath.

"Thanks, Johnny," he said. "That's some better."

He looked around. They seemed to be on the back edge of an encampment. "Can you tell me where we're at?" he said.

"Nope," said Comeaux, " 'cause I don't exactly know myself. We're somewhere south of the battlefield. That's about all I know. I hate like hell to tell you this, but your boys has drove us back."

"We won?" said Ben.

"Well," said Comeaux, "like I said, let's just say you've drove us back. There'll be another day of fighting."

"What's going to happen to me?"

"All I'm doing is just guarding you. That's all I was told. But I think we're waiting for another company to come along and join us here, and when they get here, I think we'll be moving out. That's what I think. Then I think we'll probably drop you off somewhere at some camp. That's what I think. 'Course, I don't know."

"Prison camp?" said Ben.

"Well," said Comeaux, "you're a prisoner, ain't you?"

Dhu thought it must be about noon, judging from the protestations of his stomach. He thought about killing something to eat, but that seemed like too dangerous a proposition. Someone might hear the shot. Then he would have to clean his victim, build a fire, and cook it. Someone might see the smoke. No, he decided, he would keep moving. Sooner or later he would find some food. He plodded on, silently cursing the white man for bringing his war into the Cherokee Nation. This is not my war, he thought. Not mine. He remembered the family and the home that once had been his, all gone, all victims of this white man's war.

Then he heard horses and wagons and clanking swords. He stopped and listened. The sounds seemed to be drawing nearer, and he realized there must be a road close by. He made his way through the trees in the direction of the sounds, and soon he found the road. He backed up into the tangled brush to watch a Confederate troop pass by. It wasn't any of the Indian regiments; he would have recognized them. Nor did he think that it was the Texans. Hunger gnawed at his guts, and he thought about rushing out into the road to meet them, to beg for food. He could have told them he was one of their own, and he would only have been telling half a lie. But something held him back. He watched as the last of the soldiers walked past him and moved on down the road — the last but one.

"Stand up real slow," said a voice behind him.

Dhu stood up slowly, still clutching the shotgun.

"Drop that gun."

Dhu dropped it and held his empty hands out to his sides. The Remington revolver was still tucked into the waistband of his trousers beneath his jacket.

"All right," said his captor. "Turn around and let me look at you."

Dhu turned slowly. A white man in a ragged gray uniform stood facing him, a single-shot breech-loading rifle in his hands. The rifle was pointed at Dhu's chest. Its hammer was cocked. The soldier looked at Dhu curiously.

"You one of ours," he said, "ain't you? Them Yankees all got uniforms. All of them that I seen."

Dhu could see no profit in trying to lie his way out of his sticky situation, and besides, the truth just might set him free this time. He decided to give it a try. "I was with Colonel Drew's regiment," he said. "I don't know where they are now "

"Colonel Drew? You one of them damn Indians? I guess you are, by God. You're a half-breed Indian, ain't you?"

"Yes, I am," Dhu said. "Now will you stop pointing that rifle at me?"

"Why should I?"

"We're on the same side."

"From what I heard," the rebel said, "some of you forgot that. Some of you turned on us while the fighting was going on. Some of you killed some good rebels. Even took some scalps. That's what I heard."

"Scalps?" said Dhu. He thought of Yona. Yes, he told himself. Yona might have done that. Dhu found the idea almost amusing.

"I think I'll just take you on along with me as my prisoner. We'll see what the captain thinks ought to be done about you. Get going."

Dhu turned to walk toward the road. He deliberately chose a difficult path, one that forced him to turn sideways and use his hands to brush aside brambles and low-hanging branches, and while he was doing that, he pulled out the Remington, cocked it, turned, and fired, and the rebel screamed and fell, a hole in his chest. Dhu had abandoned the shotgun when the rebel made him drop it, but he put the Remington back in the waistband of his trousers.

Dhu's shot was followed by a hubbub from the road — shouts, clattering, stamping of soldiers' feet and horses' hooves. Dhu ran back into the safety of the woods, but he could hear the sounds of pursuit. As he ran, he looked up at trees until he satisfied himself that he had found a likely refuge: a tall and stately walnut.

He embraced the walnut like a lover. He wrapped both arms around its trunk, spread his legs, and pressed his body in tight, then inched his way up until he could clutch a sturdy branch. From there the tree became a twisted, crooked ladder. He climbed until he could go no farther, until the branches up above would be too small to hold his weight and the thickness of the lush layers of leaves below would render him invisible to the eyes of anyone, blue or gray, who prowled around down there.

He was able to position himself with a tolerable degree of comfort. He could remain in the tree indefinitely, he thought, except that he felt uncommonly hungry. He would wait up there for a while, at least until there were no more sounds of searchers down below. Once he heard a shout, and once he heard men rustling through the brush below. A gray squirrel chattered indignantly at him from a neighboring tree. The blue jays scolded boldly. He relaxed and settled into the gentle cradling arms of the old walnut, thinking about the ironies of life and love and war. He admonished himself for being a misplaced philosopher, then dismissed that thought to return to his current predicament. He had marched into the battle just a day or so ago, and he hadn't known which side he was on, not really. Now the battle was apparently over, and he had managed to avoid it almost altogether. Yet he had killed twice. He wondered how long he would have to play treed coon before the woods below would be safe again for traveling.

He slept.

3

Dhu's perch in the tree soon became uncomfortable. He could still hear soldiers milling around below, cursing loudly. Dhu realized that his right leg had gone to sleep, but he was afraid to move. He tried wiggling his toes inside his boot, but that didn't help much. At last he heard a welcome command from somewhere beneath his protective layers of branches and leaves.

"Come on. Let's go."

A few complaining voices answered the command, and Dhu heard much rustling of brush and dried leaves. Then it was quiet again. Still he waited. He wanted to be sure, but he didn't want to wait long enough for another group to come along. He moved his leg, and the painful tingling rushed up and down its length. He decided to abandon the tree. The right leg was hard to control, and he had to move cautiously. He slowly made it to the floor of the forest. He pulled the captured pistol from the waistband of his trousers and looked around. There was no sign of other human life. As he started to walk toward the road, his right leg seemed to step higher than it should and to fling itself forward, then flop down unnaturally on the ground before him. Then when he stepped forward with his left, the right would almost buckle under him. He moved ahead slowly with this ungainly gait for several steps before the circulation in his right leg finally returned and he could walk normally.

He would go back to the road. His sense of direction was almost nonexistent in the thick woods, but the road would lead him somewhere. Out from under the trees he could look at the sun and determine his direction from its position in the sky. He wanted to go south and east, mostly east. He longed to be back in the Cherokee Nation. The white man's war was raging there, too, it was true, but at least he knew the territory. He knew the communities and the people, and he knew, he thought, where he could hide and safely avoid being drawn back into this conflict. The road was there, just ahead. Dhu stepped out and looked up for the sun.

"Drop your gun," came a voice.

"Put your hands up over your head."

He dropped the revolver and raised his hands. Four soldiers in gray stood up from hiding places just beside the road. There were two on either side of the road, two ahead of him, two behind him. He had walked into a trap.

Ben Lacey was sitting on the ground, his hands still tied securely behind his back. Private Johnny Comeaux was still standing guard over him when the soldiers rode up leading another prisoner. Ben looked up. He saw four mounted rebels. One, a captain riding a proud-stepping black stallion, presented a dashing and imposing figure. In the midst of the battle-weary, dirty soldiers, he appeared to be immaculate. His gray uniform looked fresh. His brass shone. A shiny black belt around his waist held an 1860 Army Colt in an army regulation holster on his right hip. From his left side a gleaming saber dangled and clattered as he moved. His full beard and short hair were dark brown with a reddish hue, and he wore a wide-brimmed black hat set at a rakish angle, its crown decorated with the feathers of cocks.

Behind him rode a cavalry sergeant and a corporal, and taking up the rear was another corporal. The corporal in the rear was leading a prisoner by a long rope tied to his saddle horn at one end and to the prisoner's wrists at the other.

The hooves of the captain's horse kicked up clouds of dust that hovered over the ground. Ben tried to hold his breath until the air cleared, but he was unable to wait that long. He breathed in the dust and felt it clog his throat and lungs.

The captain shot a piercing glance at Ben, then glanced over his shoulder toward the sergeant. "Bring the prisoner forward," he said.

"Yes, sir," said the sergeant. He looked back toward the corporal with the prisoner. "Bring him on up here," he said.

The corporal pulled the prisoner forward until he stood beside the captain's big black stallion.

Ben looked at the prisoner, who wore no uniform. His civilian clothing was dirty and torn. The man had near black hair cut straight just above his shoulders. Ben couldn't be sure, because the man was dirty, but his face appeared to be bruised and bloody. It looked to Ben as if the soldiers had beaten the man. He wondered about the man's lack of uniform and why he had been so badly mistreated. And there was something else about which to wonder: it was in the features of the man's face. . . .

Just then the captain slipped his foot out of the stirrup and kicked the prisoner hard between his shoulders. The prisoner sprawled face down in the dirt a few feet from where Ben sat. The sergeant and the two corporals laughed. The corporal with the rope loosed its end from his saddle horn and pitched it at the prisoner. The captain wheeled his black around and rode away, followed obediently by the other three. The new prisoner lay still for a moment, then crawled painfully to his knees. He barely glanced at the guard or the other prisoner. He sat back on the ground, drew up his knees, and rested his arms on them, his head hanging down to hide his face.

"Hey, Ben," said Comeaux. "Did you see that?"

"How could I miss?" said Ben.

"That was Old Harm himself."

"Old Harm? The captain?"

"Hell yes, boy. The captain. Old Harm. Captain Gordon Early. He's one the best soldiers the Confederacy has got. They call him Old Harm 'cause that's what he'll give the other side. Hot damn. I only seen him once or twice before."

Ben looked at the new prisoner, at his battered condition, and he thought, Old Harm sounds about right. He was glad he had not been captured by Old Harm. Then he looked back at his guard. "Johnny," he said.

"Yeah?"

"This fellow looks to me like he could use a drink of water. Maybe a little to wash his face, too."

Comeaux stepped over to the battered prisoner and nudged him with a foot. The man hardly responded.

"Hey there," said Comeaux. "You, boy. You want some water?"

The man raised his head and looked up at Comeaux.

"My God," said Comeaux. "They did kick the shit out of you, didn't they? Come on."

He took hold of the rope and pulled, helping the man to his feet, and he led him over to the water barrel. He pointed to the dipper.

"Help yourself," he said.

The man drank and poured water over his head. He tried to wash his face, but his wrists were still bound and he had no rag. He only managed to clean his face a little. Mostly he just smeared the blood and dirt around. Comeaux gestured toward the spot near Ben where the man had been sitting, and the prisoner went back and sat again on the ground.

"What's your name, boy?" said Comeaux.

The man raised his head again and looked at the guard.

"Hey," said Comeaux, "I'm just trying to be friendly. We got to sit here and keep each other company whether we like it or not. I'm Johnny Comeaux from Louisiana, and your fellow prisoner there is Ben Lacey. He's from Iowa. What's your name?"

"Roderick Dhu Walker."

"Roderick Doo?" said Comeaux. "I ain't never heard a name like that before, except for the Walker part. I've knowed some Walkers. But I ain't never heard of no Roderick Doo. Have you ever heard that before, Ben?"

"No," said Ben. "I never."

"What kind of name is that?" said Comeaux.

"It's Scottish," said Dhu.

"Scottish?" said Comeaux. "Are you a Scotchman?"

"I'm part Scottish," said Dhu. "My father was fond of Sir Walter Scott, particularly *The Lady of the Lake*."

"What?" said Comeaux.

"That's where the name came from.

Roderick Dhu. He's a character in *The Lady of the Lake*."

"Oh," said Ben. "I get it. It's a story. Right?"

"It's a poem that tells a story," said Dhu.

"You're named after a character in a poem?" said Ben. "Well, I never heard of that before. Me, I'm named after a President. Benjamin Franklin."

Dhu looked at Ben. He opened his mouth to correct Ben, but changed his mind. He was obviously surrounded by ignorance. He decided to let it go.

"Where you from, Rod— uh, Walker?" said Comeaux.

Dhu looked up at the guard. A real redneck, he thought. If he told the man the truth, he'd probably get another beating. On the other hand, everyone in the camp would surely know soon. What the hell. "The Cherokee Nation," he said.

"Indian Territory?" said Comeaux.

"If that's what you want to call it."

"You an Indian?" said Ben.

"I'm Cherokee," Dhu said.

"You said you was a damned Scotchman," said Comeaux. "That's where you got that funny name."

"I said I'm part Scottish," said Dhu, "and I am."

"A half-breed," said Comeaux. "Ben, you know what you got there for a partner? We got some Indian troops from over in the Indian Territory. Some of them turned on us when they got into the fight. Turned traitor, that's what they did. What do you think about that?"

"I come down here from Iowa to fight you Johnny Rebs," said Ben, "but I got no use for a traitor, no matter what side he's on."

"I'm on no side," said Dhu. "This is not my war."

Ben looked sideways at Dhu and squinted. "I never seen an Indian before," he said.

The guard changed, and the new guard wasn't as friendly as Comeaux had been. He had the same kind of southern drawl, but he didn't ask where the prisoners had come from or what their names were. Instead he asked why they didn't get up and try to run away so he could shoot them in the back. He told them he had better things to do with his time than to stand guard over a damn Yankee and a murderous, traitorous, scalping Indian. When they didn't respond to his verbal abuse, he kicked them or struck them with the butt of his rifle. When night fell and they tried to sleep, he kept them awake.

"If I can't sleep, you can't sleep," he said.

The next morning the whole camp woke early and prepared to march. The other end of the long rope that bound Dhu's wrists was tied to Ben's, and they began to march. Dhu noticed they were heading east, moving even farther away from his home. He felt a sudden sinking hopelessness in his stomach. There were soldiers on horseback and soldiers afoot, soldiers driving wagons and others riding in the wagons. Ben and Dhu, of course, always walked. Because of the way in which they were tied together, Ben was ahead of Dhu. Now and then soldiers behind Dhu would prod him along with a kick, a blow, a nudge of a rifle butt, or the prod of a bayonet. Dhu found himself wondering about his parents and others of their generation who had suffered the forced march from Georgia, Alabama, North Carolina, and Tennessee that was known to the world as the Trail Where They Cried or the Trail of Tears. The Cherokees called it *ahuhsidasdi*, to move things about, or *digejiluhstanuh*, the way they were herded down there away from where they wanted to be. Thinking of their ordeal gave Dhu strength. Old men and women and children had been forced to make that other long walk. He was a young man; he could take it.

He looked at the back of the young Iowan ahead of him and wondered how he managed to get his strength. What memories had he to draw on for inspiration? The thought lasted only a moment. He told himself he had no interest in the white man. It was the U.S. government that had driven his people west in the first place. The United States had broken its promise to protect the Cherokees from invasion. They had allowed the Confederates to come in and force Chief Ross to sign a treaty with them. It was the fault of the United States that Dhu and the other Cherokees had been conscripted into the Confederate army and marched into Arkansas. It was the fault of the United States that Dhu was walking along a strange road with his hands tied, eating the dust of Confederate soldiers. He didn't care about the ignorant Iowan who had been named after Benjamin Franklin and thought that he had been named for a President.

No one had actually told Ben how the

battle had turned out, but he had overheard snatches of conversation between the rebel soldiers. The rebels had lost. They were retreating. Ben's feelings over that news were mixed. Of course, he told himself, he was glad to learn that his side had won. But marching along with his hands tied behind his back and a turncoat Indian tied behind him, he didn't feel as if he had been on the winning side. He wanted to shout at his captors. *Hey, I won. Turn me loose.* For the first time in his life he felt a strong sense of an overwhelming, indifferent, and unfair universe. Suddenly he had a sense that the rebel soldiers were not even responsible for his situation. It was as if they were not even there. It was just him and cold chance, and he felt like shouting out to it and cursing it for the cruel trick it had played on him. But he didn't. He trudged on.

They stopped briefly at noon, or sometime thereabouts, for a rest and a meal. Ben and Dhu were each given a plate of beans and a cup of water. Nothing more. They were untied and kept under heavy guard just long enough to eat and be taken to the woods to relieve themselves. Then they were retied as they had been before, and the march soon was resumed. The afternoon passed as had the morning: no one spoke to Ben or Dhu except to shout brief and hurried commands: "Get going." "Hurry up there." "Move along." Nor did the prisoners speak to each other. The rope that connected them was at least twenty feet long. Ben did not look back to see how Dhu was making it. Most of the time Dhu looked at the ground in front of him, only occasionally glancing up at the Yankee's back, twenty feet ahead.

Late that evening they made a full camp for the night. Tents were pitched and fires were built. Dhu and Ben were again served beans and water. A new guard watched over them. He was not as friendly as Comeaux, but he was not cruel, either. He was indifferent. At least, he seemed to be. The weary prisoners thought that they might at least get to sleep that night. There was a slight chill in the March night air as they stretched out, without blankets, on the hard ground. Even so, they welcomed the rest, however brief. They were startled out of their sleep by the rush of a horse's hooves. They sat up to find a big black stallion stamping around between them. On its back was Old Harm.

"Get up!" hc shouted. "Private, get these prisoners to their feet."

Ben and Dhu stood up, Ben with difficulty because his hands were tied behind his back. The private, responding to Captain Early's command, helped Ben up with a jerk. Early's horse still stamped around. Ben and Dhu stood and waited, wondering what the captain was up to.

"Sergeant!" shouted Early.

"Yes, sir."

The sergeant who had been with Old Harm when they had seen him before came riding up.

"Gather the men up in a circle right around here," said Early. "We're going to have some entertainment tonight."

Dhu looked up, and he saw that Old Harm's gaze was fixed intently on him.

4

They were surrounded by a ring of gray-suited soldiers. There was a fire in the middle of the ring. Old Harm still sat in his saddle, and the black stallion pranced around just inside the ring. Dhu and Ben, their hands still tied, wondered what the captain had planned for them.

"Private," said Early to the guard, "untie the prisoners."

"Yes, sir." The private untied Dhu and Ben.

"Give me that rope," said Early.

The private handed Old Harm the rope, and the captain began to coil it up. Ben and Dhu were both rubbing their wrists, trying to get the circulation back in them. Old Harm quit coiling when he had only about three feet of rope left dangling. He turned the stallion and urged him toward Dhu. The big horse didn't seem to know how to walk. He moved in fits and starts and jerks. He lunged toward Dhu, then stopped just short of running him down and pranced nervously. In spite of himself, Dhu backed up a step.

"Walker," said Early, looking down contemptuously. "You were with Colonel Drew's regiment."

"Yes," said Dhu. "I was."

Early lashed out with the rope, burning a stripe across Dhu's right cheek.

"Did Colonel Drew teach you how to address an officer?" he said.

"Yes, sir," said Dhu. The cheek burned, and the burn went deep. Dhu thought about the two rebels he had killed. He had not wanted to kill them. Marching to Pea Ridge from the Cherokee Nation, he had not wanted to kill anyone. That had changed: he now wanted to kill Captain Gordon Early in the worst possible way. The only problem was, Old Harm was just liable to kill him first.

"It seems," said Early, "that you boys forgot who it was you were supposed to be fighting. You came here to fight Yanks. But you didn't do that, did you? You killed rebels, good Confederate soldiers. Southern boys."

Old Harm had worked himself into a frenzy, and to punctuate his last phrase, he lashed out with the rope again. This time Dhu saw the blow coming and got an arm up in time to protect his face.

"Well," continued Early, "maybe you just

didn't know any better, you being an ignorant Indian. But we're going to teach you better. You see that man right there? Your fellow prisoner? He's a Yankee. See his blue suit? That's who you're supposed to be fighting. Now fight him."

Dhu looked at Ben. He looked back at Old Harm incredulously.

"Fight him," Old Harm said. "Now."

Dhu stood there, a look of disbelief on his face. He had no particular liking for the ignorant farm boy, but he did not want to fight him, certainly not for the pleasure of a bunch of rednecks and one sadistic Confederate officer.

"Fight!" shouted Early. He lashed Dhu with the rope again and again. "Fight that damn Yankee or I'll beat you to death!"

Ben stood nervously watching the beating. He wondered why Dhu didn't attack him, why he just stood there taking the beating. Finally he could stand it no longer. He rushed forward and swung a right, which caught Dhu a glancing blow on the chin. It was not a powerful blow, but it did get Dhu's attention. It also got the attention of Early, who quit swinging his rope. Dhu stepped back and put his hands up in a defensive posture, and Ben swung again. Dhu warded off the blow, and Ben jabbed with his left. Dhu knocked the left jabs aside with ease, then swung a right that caught Ben on the side of the head and staggered him. Ben shook his head to clear it and felt anger suddenly come upon him. He had started this fight to stop the beating, but Dhu's unexpected blow made him mad. He ducked his head and rushed at Dhu like a mad bull. Dhu tried to step aside, but Ben flung out an arm and caught him around the waist. They clenched and pounded each other's ribs.

The soldiers were all shouting, some for Ben and some for Dhu. Bets were being made. The fighters' feet became tangled, and they fell heavily to the ground and rolled through the fire. Ben screamed as he felt the flames on his back, and the shouts and laughter from the crowd became deafening. When the two prisoners stopped rolling, Ben was on top, and he flailed with both fists at Dhu's head. Dhu covered his face with both arms, then bucked, throwing Ben forward. While Ben was still off balance, Dhu wriggled out from under him and got back to his feet. He backed off and waited for the Yankee to get up.

"Get him, Yank!" a soldier shouted.

"Kill him, Indian!" yelled another.

The two circled each other, fists up, ready to swing. Just then a booming voice cut through all the other noise.

"Captain Early, what is the meaning of this?"

The crowd grew silent. Early looked down from the back of his stallion at the gray-bearded colonel who had just shouldered his way through the crowd.

"Just a little entertainment for the troops, sir," he said. "No harm done."

"Get all these men back to their tents. There will be no more entertainment," the colonel said. "I'll see you in my tent, Captain."

"Yes, sir."

The crowd dispersed in a remarkably short time. Dhu and Ben stood facing each other across the fire. The private, their guard, stood there fidgeting. The colonel looked over the scene.

"Get these men cleaned up and bedded down," he said.

"Yes, sir," said the guard.

The next morning they packed up early, and again they walked. Once Old Harm rode past the two prisoners and gave them a look of scorn, but he said nothing. They walked some more. Both Dhu and Ben were bruised from the fight, and the walking was slightly more painful than it had been the day before. But they weren't tied, and they didn't complain. They thought of the colonel as their savior. They expected to be treated better in the future.

At noon they stopped again, and this time their beans included a little pork, and each of them was given a hard biscuit and a cup of hot coffee.

Then Early rode up again. "Private," he said, "if those men have finished their meal, tie them up again."

"Yes, sir."

"Just like they were before." Old Harm jerked the reins and turned the black stallion. He was gone as quickly as he had appeared.

Without a word the private tied Ben's hands behind his back once more and bound Dhu's hands in front of him. Soon they were walking along the road again, breathing the dust of the troops ahead. Dhu thought about the fight the night before, and he thought about the sadistic captain known as Old Harm. The meal had strengthened him. The melancholy he had been suffering, the sense of hopelessness, was gone. It had been replaced by anger and a determination to do something about his situation. He had to escape. He had to find a way to get away from these rednecks. He knew he could do it. All he had to do was put his whole mind to it and watch for the right opportunity. His hands were securely bound. He cursed himself silently for not having tried to escape earlier when his hands were free.

Then he had an idea: he couldn't reach the knots that held his own wrists together, but he could untie Ben and then Ben could untie him. He would have to take the Yankee with him, and they would have to leave that night, before the army moved any farther away from the Cherokee Nation. Tonight, after dark, he would find a way to talk to Ben. They would run into the night. Dhu would go his way and Ben could go his. Back to his regiment. Back to Iowa. That was his business. Dhu would go home.

Dhu fought off an urge to catch up with Ben and tell him about his plan. Of course he couldn't do that. The soldiers would want to know what they were talking about. He would have to wait. His energy level increased with his excitement, and although he was frustrated and impatient, the thoughts, the planning, the anticipation, sustained him for the rest of the long afternoon walk. When they finally stopped and made camp for the night, he was not tired. He looked at Ben as their guard found a spot for them for the night. Ben dropped wearily to the ground. Dhu sat down close enough to Ben to talk to him, but not so close as to appear conspiratorial. There was plenty of activity in the camp while the soldiers were busy preparing things for the night. The time would never be better.

"Ben," he said.

The guard was nearby, but he was not watching them closely. He had his eyes on the activities around them. An officers' tent was being erected not far away, and the guard kept glancing toward it. Now and then he looked back at his charges. They were just sitting there on the ground. He wasn't worried about them.

Ben raised his head slowly and looked at Dhu.

"We've got to untie each other and escape," Dhu said.

Ben raised his eyebrows a little.

"Tonight."

"How?" said Ben.

The guard looked back toward his prisoners, and Dhu stared directly at him. "When do we eat?" he asked.

"You'll eat when the rest of us do," said the guard.

He turned away from Dhu with obvious irritation. That was what Dhu had hoped for.

"After dark," he said to Ben. "When everyone's asleep but our guard. We'll kill him, and we'll run."

"How do we kill him?" Ben said skeptically. He resisted the idea of being told what to do by an Indian, especially one who had turned against his own kind. Dhu reached down between his feet and picked up the rope that lay there.

"With this," he said. He made a loop in the rope.

"I don't know," said Ben.

"I'll do it. You just be ready when I make the move. That's all. Just be ready."

The officers' tent was finished, and the soldiers who had put it up left. Then the colonel who had stopped the fight appeared and went inside. It wasn't long after that the beans were dished out. There was no pork in the beans that night, but Ben and Dhu were given coffee again. Dhu finished his coffee and stretched out on the ground.

Ben was nervous. He was tied to an Indian, the first he had ever seen in his life, and the Indian was planning to kill their guard. He looked at Dhu, who appeared to have gone to sleep. Ben wondered how he could sleep at a time like this. He stood up and walked away from Dhu as far as he could go without pulling on the rope. Then he sat back down.

The guard watched him suspiciously at first, then glanced at Dhu and smirked. He apparently thought Ben didn't want to be too close to the Indian. Well, thought Ben, he's right about that. He lay down on his side and tried to get comfortable. It wasn't easy with his hands tied behind his back.

There was still plenty of camp noise, but Ben could hear distinct voices in the officers' tent. He recognized the colonel's voice and that of Captain Early. He wasn't really interested in what they were talking about, but he strained to hear anyway. It was something to do. He found that he could make out most of the conversation. After a few minutes, Early left.

The sun went down, and Ben tried to sleep, but he was too nervous. He waited, wondering when Dhu would make his move, wondering what the Indian would do and how he would do it. He heard a voice nearby and looked up. It was a changing of the guard. The private who had been guarding them was being relieved — by Johnny Comeaux. No, thought Ben. Not Johnny. Maybe the Indian wouldn't kill him after all. Maybe he wouldn't get a chance. He closed his eyes and pretended to be asleep. He didn't want to talk to Johnny that night.

5

Dhu recalled that Johnny Comeaux had been friendly with Ben. They had talked together and called each other by first names. A plan began to form in his mind. He edged, inch by inch, closer to Ben. It seemed to take forever. He didn't want to attract Comeaux's attention. Finally, when he was close enough, he put his plan into action.

"Ben," he whispered.

Ben turned his head toward Dhu.

"You're sick," said Dhu. "Real sick. Show it."

Ben was silent for a moment. He didn't know what Dhu had in mind. He didn't want Dhu to kill Comeaux, the only one of his captors who had been kind to him. But he didn't want to spend the rest of the war in a southern prison camp, either. It was his duty to try to escape. He was enough of a soldier to know that. His heart began to pound in his chest unmercifully. He became aware that he was sweating. He was afraid. He hated to admit it, even to himself, but he knew that the Indian was right: the longer they waited, the worse their chance of escape would be. They were getting deeper into rebel territory with each step. They had to act at once. He groaned.

Comeaux heard the groan and looked toward the prisoners. Ben groaned again and rolled over on the ground, pulling his knees up toward his chest. Comeaux took a couple of steps toward him.

"Ben?" he said. "That you? What's wrong, Ben?"

"I'm sick," said Ben. "It hurts real bad."

Johnny Comeaux moved in closer, and Dhu gathered up some of the slack in the rope that tied him to Ben. He formed a loop, and he watched, trying to keep his breathing quiet, waiting for just the right moment.

Comeaux walked closer to Ben. "What is it, Ben?" he said. "Is it your stomach?"

Ben groaned and rolled over again.

"Oh, God," he said, "it hurts."

Comeaux dropped to one knee and put a hand on Ben's shoulder.

Dhu sprang into action. Two long strides took him right to Comeaux's back. He slipped the noose over Comeaux's head and pulled. His wrists were bound together, so he couldn't pull the noose tight enough. He had put his hands as far down on the rope as he dared. He had to leave a big enough loop to get easily over the guard's head. In order to tighten the rope against the man's throat and keep him from crying out and spreading the alarm, he had to throw his weight against Comeaux's back and pull back on the rope.

"Ben," Dhu said. "Help me."

Ben was staring at Comeaux's face, at its horrified expression. He couldn't move. Besides, his hands were tied behind him. What could he do?

"Help me," said Dhu.

"I can't," said Ben.

Dhu shoved hard with his knees and thighs and pulled back on the rope. Comeaux tried to call out for help, but all he could manage was pitiful choking and gagging sounds. Ben began to really feel sick. It was taking too long. He stood and backed up to Comeaux and, putting his hands on Comeaux's head, bore down with all his weight, pushing Comeaux's chin into his chest. Dhu yanked viciously on the rope, and Comeaux suddenly went limp. Dhu waited a moment before relaxing. Ben was still pushing down on Johnny Comeaux's head. Dhu slowly eased up on his grip, and there was no reaction from Comeaux.

"He's dead, Ben," he said. "Let's go."

He fumbled with the rope for a moment, trying to get it unwrapped from around the neck of the lifeless body. After getting it free, he gathered up most of the slack to carry between them, since the rope was too long to be allowed to trail. He pushed Ben toward the edge of the camp, toward the darkness of the woods, toward the west.

"Let's go," he said again.

Ben tore his eyes away from the corpse that had been the private from Louisiana and ran. It was awkward running with his hands tied behind him, and once before reaching the woods, he stumbled and fell. Dhu helped him to his feet, and they ran on. Once into the woods, Ben slowed down.

"We can't stop now," said Dhu. "Come on."

They ran through tangled brush over rocky terrain, panting and stumbling. They ran into low-hanging branches and even occasionally into tree trunks that seemed to lurch in front of them. They ran until Ben thought his lungs were going to burst. Then Dhu stopped.

"Come here," he said, panting, gasping for breath. "Let's try to get this rope off."

Dhu began working at the knots on

Ben's wrists. It was slow and tedious, but as he worked the knots loose, his breath slowly returned to him. At last Ben's wrists were free. Dhu thrust his hands toward Ben, and Ben untied the knots. Then they sat down, leaning back against a tree and breathing deeply.

"They'll be after us," said Ben.

"I know," Dhu said.

"How soon, you reckon?"

"I don't know," said Dhu. "It depends on how soon they find out we're gone. If they don't discover it until morning, we've got a damn good chance of getting away clean. Even if they find out tonight, they might not try to hunt us down in the dark. If we keep going all night, we ought to make it all right. We'll have to watch out for other patrols, though."

"If they do catch us," Ben said, "they'll likely just shoot us down."

"Especially if that sadistic bastard Old Harm is in charge," Dhu said.

"He won't be," said Ben, "but it don't matter. Any of them will kill us after what we done to Johnny."

Dhu cocked his head and looked curiously toward Ben. He couldn't see anything of the other man except a silhouette in the dark woods. "What do you mean,

Old Harm won't be with them?" he said.

"Earlier, when Old Harm went into the colonel's tent, I could hear what they was talking about," Ben told him. "The colonel sent Old Harm off on a special assignment. The orders came from somewhere else. He's already gone. Gone to Texas."

"Texas?" said Ben. "What's he going to do down there?"

"I couldn't make out everything, but it sounded to me like some foreign government is sending a bunch of gold to the rebels. It's coming through Mexico, and Old Harm's got to go get it and bring it back."

"Are you sure about that?"

"Yeah," said Ben. "I heard that much."

"Where in Texas?"

"I don't know. I never heard that."

They sat in silence for a long moment. The darkness seemed overwhelming, its silence broken only by the songs of night birds and bugs.

"Where you going from here?" said Dhu.

Ben didn't answer right away.

"I don't know," he said finally. "I don't even know where the hell I'm at. I guess I'll have to follow you along for a while. Maybe come daylight I can figure something out."

"We ought to go after that gold," said

Dhu.

"What?"

"Do you want the Confederacy to get that gold? Nobody else on our side knows about it. We ought to stop Old Harm."

"I don't even know which side you're on," said Ben.

"Well, then, I'll tell you," Dhu said. "To begin with, the Cherokee Nation didn't want anything to do with this war. It's a white man's war, not ours. We've got a treaty with the United States that promised to protect us from invasion, and our chief and our council were determined to stay out of the war. But some Cherokee citizens joined with the South. It had nothing to do with the Cherokee Nation; they did it on their own. They raised up a pretty good army and set out to make the rest of us join them. So some of us organized to fight them off, because we couldn't get the United States to send any troops down to protect our neutrality. We called ourselves the Pins. Some called us Union Indians, and I guess in a way we are — or were — because we were fighting against the Confederates. But what we really wanted was just to stay out of the war. Do you follow me?"

"Well, yeah," Ben said, "but you were

with the Confederate army."

"The United States never sent troops down to help us like they were supposed to, so the Confederate Cherokees finally forced our chief to sign a treaty with them. One day they told us we were Confederates. Just like that. They said we'd just changed sides, and we were going into battle. That's when they marched us to Pea Ridge. I never was a Confederate. Neither were any of the other Pins."

Again they sat in silence for a while. Ben was mulling all this information over in his head.

"Did you kill any Union soldiers during the battle?" he said.

"No."

"Did you kill any rebels?"

"Two," Dhu said. "Three now. I tried to stay out of it, but two rebel soldiers came up on me in the woods. It was them or me."

"I never knew an Indian before," Ben said.

"You don't know me," Dhu said. "What about Old Harm and the gold?"

"I'll think about it. I'll let you know."

"Well, I guess you've got the rest of the night to think about it, but you'd better make a decision by morning."

"Texas is a big state," said Ben. "We'd never find him."

"Can't you remember anything else that was said? The name of a town? Anything?"

Ben scratched his head and wrinkled his face. "The Texas Road," he said. "He'll go down and come back on the Texas Road."

"I know where that is," Dhu said. "We could do it, Ben. We could stop him."

"I don't know."

Dhu let out a heavy sigh and felt a pang in his ribs where Ben had hit him during the fight forced by Old Harm.

"Ben?" he said.

"Yeah?"

"How come you came at me the other night?"

"You mean the fight?"

"Yeah. How come?"

"I don't know," Ben said. "I guess it just seemed like the only way to stop Old Harm from beating you with the rope."

"We could stop him again, Ben. If you don't want to think of it as a patriotic thing to do, think of it as getting back at Old Harm for what he did to us, for what he'll do to other men he might get his hands on in the future."

"He is a mean-spirited man," said Ben.

"He's a sadist," said Dhu.

"What's that mean?"

"He gets pleasure out of hurting people."

"Oh, yeah. I guess he is that. How come you're so smart?"

"I went to school," said Dhu.

"I didn't know Indians had schools."

"I imagine there's a lot you don't know," Dhu said. He started to leave it at that, but then he added, "About Indians."

"I didn't get very far in school," Ben said. "I was needed at home on the farm. I had enough book-learning to work a farm — or to be a soldier. A private, anyway. I guess you need book-learning to be an officer."

"No, just influence," said Dhu. "You need influence and money."

"What do you mean?"

"Ah, never mind," Dhu said. "I guess a good education might do it, too. Right now I wish I had a good cup of coffee, but I guess we'd better get started. Come on."

Traveling through the woods was much easier without the rope tied to their wrists and strung out between them, and the tension between them was not as bad as before. They had talked more sitting there in the woods than in the entire time they had spent together as prisoners. They didn't really like each other, but at least they knew each other a little better. Each knew that the other was human.

Dhu led the way through the woods, and Ben followed. Dhu didn't tell Ben that his sense of direction in these Arkansas woods was probably no better than the Iowa farm boy's. He decided to swing around and find the road again. They should be far enough away from the Confederate troops, and the going, especially at night, would be much easier along the road. He turned in the direction he thought the road would be. Soon he wondered if he had made a mistake. Maybe the road was off in some other direction altogether. But he didn't let Ben know he was unsure. It wouldn't be right, he thought, to let a white man know that an Indian had lost his sense of direction. He kept going, and soon he found the road. He stepped out onto it as if he had known where it was all along.

"Here we are," he said. "Let's take a rest."

They sat down on the edge of the road, and Dhu lay back in the deep grass. Now that they were out from under the trees, he could see the sky clearly. He located the group of stars the Cherokees called It Moves West During Winter, which the white man called the Big Dipper. He used that to find You See It Early in the Morning, or the North Star. He stood up.

"You ready to go?" he asked Ben.

"Yeah," the Iowan answered wearily.

"This way." Dhu led the way with confidence, but Ben didn't just follow along anymore; he walked beside Dhu. They walked maybe five minutes like that in silence before Ben spoke up.

"Dhu," he said.

"Yeah."

"I'll do it. I'll go with you to get the gold, to stop Old Harm." As soon as he had said the words, he was sorry. Couldn't he have kept his mouth shut just a little longer? At least until morning? Damn. He wasn't really sure he wanted to get himself any more deeply involved with that Indian than he already was. Dhu didn't answer, and Ben didn't say any more. They walked on in silence.

6

Ben and Dhu had been silent for some time, a half an hour, forty-five minutes. Ben didn't know, but he picked up the conversation as if no time had passed.

"Dhu," he said, "how we going to steal that gold from Old Harm anyway? We got no guns. No horses. We ain't got nothing."

"We'll get them, Ben."

They continued walking along the road at a steady pace while they talked. Their panting gave the sentences they spoke unusual patterns of punctuation.

"Where?" Ben asked. "Where we going to get horses and guns? How we going to get them?"

"If we don't run across some we can steal along the way," said Dhu, "I've got friends in the Cherokee Nation. They'll get them for us."

"We going into the Cherokee Nation?"

"It's the closest place," said Dhu, "and the safest."

"Is there any white people in there?"

"Don't worry. We won't scalp you."

"You scalped some men back there in

the battle," Ben said.

"I didn't scalp anyone."

"But some of the Indians did. That's what I heard."

"You believe everything you hear? Besides, what if they did? A dead man doesn't care anymore what happens to him."

"I don't know about this," Ben said.

Dhu stopped suddenly and turned on Ben. "Go on, then," he said. "Go wherever you want to go. I'm not forcing you to come with me. Go on."

Ben tried to stare at Dhu, but it was dark, and he saw only a shape before him in the road. "I don't know where else to go," he said. "Hell, I don't know where we're at."

Dhu started walking again, and Ben fell in step.

They walked along in silence for several minutes before Ben spoke again. "I don't know how we're going to steal any gold, if we don't find something to eat. We'll starve to death before we can get anywhere."

Dhu swallowed a sharp response to Ben's last comment. They had eaten supper, and it was not yet breakfast time. Ben was not starving; he was just grumbling. Dhu thought he might be better off if he got rid of Ben and did the job alone or with some other Pin Indians from the Cherokee Nation. He didn't need this Iowa farm boy, this Yankee foot soldier, this whining, grumbling white boy. But how could he get rid of him? Kill him? No. He had sworn he wouldn't kill Yankees. He could just run off and leave him to fend for himself, but would Ben be able to survive alone? He would not be likely to find other Yankee soldiers, and if he ran into civilians or rebel soldiers, which was very likely, he would be a goner. Dhu decided that running off and leaving Ben would be the same as killing him. He would just have to put up with him for a while. He would wait and see how things went. And when Ben said something stupid, he would just ignore it.

Ben, too, walked along in silence. He had said something and had not been answered. That was an insult, he thought, and the insult had come from an Indian. His face burned with emotion, but he could not quite put a name to the emotion. What had he expected Dhu to say? Ben knew they were not starving. They had not yet missed a meal. He thought they probably would miss a meal, maybe several meals. He should have stated his complaint differently, he decided. He wasn't good with words. He wasn't smart, but that wasn't his fault; his father had pulled him out of school to work on the farm. But just the same, he was a white man, and it wasn't right that he should be put down by an Indian.

"I didn't mean I'm starving right now," he blurted out suddenly. "I just meant that we're going to have to find something to eat sometime. That's all I meant."

"We'll find something when the time comes," said Dhu.

Well, thought Ben, at least it was a response.

They walked throughout the night. Once, as they passed a house, a dog barked. It gave them a fright, but no one came out of the house to investigate. They hurried on down the road. They did not encounter anyone or anything else on the road that night. When the sun came up, they slipped off the road and into the woods and found a spot to rest.

"It would probably be best if we didn't both sleep at the same time," Dhu said. "I'll watch first."

After a short while Ben stirred and declared that he was awake. Dhu stretched out on the ground and took a fitful nap. Both men were hungry and nervous, and in spite of the fact that they had spent the night walking, they found that they couldn't sleep well. They decided to search for something to eat. Dhu thought maybe he could find some berries or nuts, maybe even some edible mushrooms or ramps or watercress — anything that they could eat raw without much preparation. But it was a little too early in the spring, and Dhu could not find anything. They decided to move on.

In the daylight they traveled much more cautiously. They couldn't risk being seen. If they ran into Union troops, Ben would be all right, but Dhu couldn't risk being seen by anyone until he was safe in Pin country.

It was late morning when they came across the house. It couldn't really be called a farmhouse, since the land around it showed no sign of cultivation. It was just a small house beside the road. The woods grew up close to it on three sides. The house looked as if it had been there for a good long while, as did the old man sitting on the small porch in a cane-bottomed chair, smoking a corncob pipe, an old hound dog sleeping beside his chair. Dhu and Ben stopped. They looked at each other, then back at the farmhouse. Smoke rose lazily from a rock chimney at the near end of the little house.

"Do we take to the woods to get around him?" asked Ben, his voice low.

"I don't know," Dhu said. "He doesn't look too dangerous to me. What do you think?"

"There might be someone else in the house."

"Likely an old woman."

"Maybe kids?" Ben said. "Maybe big kids. Grown boys. Men. With guns."

"Maybe," Dhu said, "but not likely. Grown boys would likely have been conscripted."

"Likely," said Ben.

They looked at each other again.

"It ain't cold just now," Ben said.

"No."

"Then that there's a cooking fire."

"Likely," Dhu said.

"Let's chance it."

They walked on down to the house. The old man raised his eyebrows when he saw them coming. He made no other sign until they were right in front of his house. "Howdy," he said then.

Dhu thought that the old man looked

suspicious. He nodded. "Howdy," he said. "My name's Dhu Walker. My partner here is Ben Lacey."

"They call me Elder Coon," said the old man. "It could be a mite dangerous walking around in these parts in that there blue suit."

"Yeah," Ben said. "I know that."

"You ain't a spy, are you?"

"I wouldn't be a very good one dressed like this."

"Nope. I reckon not."

Elder Coon took a few puffs on his pipe and looked at Dhu. "You a Yankee, too?" he asked.

"I'm a Cherokee," Dhu said. "I was conscripted into the service of the Confederacy."

Elder Coon's eyes flicked from Ben to Dhu. "A Yankee and a rebel," he said. He gave a little laugh. "Deserters?"

"Would it matter to you?" Dhu said.

"Not to me. I got no use for the damn war. I got two growed boys. When I seen this war a-coming, I give them all the money I had in the world. It warn't much, but I give it to them. Give them all the guns in the house. All except an old scattergun. Told them to hightail it out of here. Go west. To hell with the damn war, both sides. Sure enough, gray-suited soldier boys come riding up here hunting my boys. I told them they was too late. Told them my boys had gone to Californee looking for gold. I don't know where my boys are. If this damn war ever gets over, I reckon they'll come on back home."

Dhu stepped forward a couple of steps. "The truth is, Mr. Coon, we escaped from a rebel camp last night. We were prisoners. We've been walking all night and all this morning, trying to get on over to the Cherokee Nation to get away from the war."

"We're awful hungry," said Ben.

Coon puffed at his pipe, but the fire had gone out. He reached down and tapped the bowl on the edge of his chair and then tucked the pipe into a pocket of his loose-fitting trousers. Then he heaved himself up from his chair.

"Well," he said, "come on in. Might find something."

Ben and Dhu followed Coon into the house. The old hound stood up and moved around to the other side of the chair as they passed him by. That was the first sign of life he had displayed. Inside, Coon began rummaging around shelves and cupboards. There was no one else in the house.

"You live here alone, Mr. Coon?" said Dhu.

"Now that my boys is gone I do," said Coon. He had found some coffee and was dumping some into a pan of water. "My wife died a few years ago. Buried her out back. Now and again I get to thinking I ought to hunt me a new one."

He chuckled as he placed the pan of water with the coffee grounds in it on the fire.

"We'll let that boil up," he said, "and I'll find us something to eat."

The old man was not a good cook, but Dhu and Ben ate heartily of his boiled potatoes, hard, cold biscuits, and salt pork. They drank all of the boiled coffee.

"You boys look to me like you could stand a rest," Coon said. "Stretch out in here and relax. I'll go back out on the porch and keep a watch for you. If anyone comes along the road, I'll step on my old dog's tail. You hear him howl, you slip out the back door and into the woods."

He went outside, not waiting for an answer. Dhu and Ben exchanged a glance, then found a place to lie down. They slept into the middle of the afternoon, and then Elder Coon made more coffee and prepared another meal. It was almost identical to the first one, except that this time he added some greens. After they had eaten, Coon dragged out an old trunk and opened it. He rummaged around in it until he found an old shirt and a pair of trousers. He handed them to Ben.

"They ain't much," he said, "but they won't get you killed near as quick as them that you're a wearing."

When Ben had changed his clothes, he held the blue uniform up in front of him.

"What'll I do with this?" he said.

"Give it here," said Coon. He took the uniform and carried it to the fireplace. "Best thing I know to do with any soldier suit," he said, and he tossed it into the fire.

"Mr. Coon," Dhu said, "we surely do appreciate your kind hospitality, but I'm afraid we're going to have to hit the trail again."

"You're probably right," said Coon. "Just a minute."

He rummaged in a cupboard and soon handed a bag of hard biscuits and jerky to Dhu. "It's the best I can offer," he said. "Good luck to you. If you ever find yourselves in this part of the country again, stop by and see if I'm still alive."

"Yes, sir," said Dhu. "I surely will." He offered his hand, and the old man took it.

"Me, too," Ben said. "I hope to see you again."

Outside again, they walked down the road. When they had gotten well beyond the house, Dhu turned to face Ben and started to laugh.

"What?" said Ben. "What the hell's the matter with you?"

"You sure do look peculiar in Elder Coon's hand-me-downs," said Dhu.

"Well," said Ben, a pout forming on his face, "you don't look so good yourself, and when I change clothes again I'll look better, but I don't think a new outfit would help you none."

Dhu laughed and walked on ahead. Ben waited until Dhu had gotten a few steps ahead of him before he started walking, and he stayed several paces behind. They hadn't gone far when Dhu slowed and turned back toward Ben.

"That old Coon," he said, "was a pretty nice fellow, wasn't he?"

Ben was taken by surprise. He wasn't really ready for friendly conversation just yet. "Yeah," he said, "he was."

"Elder Coon," said Dhu. He gave a little laugh. "It almost sounds like an Indian name."

"Well, it don't sound nothing like your name," said Ben.

"Dhu Walker is my English name," said Dhu. "I have another name that's my Indian name."

"What is it?" said Ben.

Dhu walked on a few steps before answering. "Never mind," he said. "You don't need to know."

7

They crept up a hill on their bellies, and when they reached the top, they slowly raised their heads to look over and down on a big house. A barn and a corral stood behind the house, and in the corral they could see four fine-looking horses.

"That's Boyd Carr's house," said Dhu. "He's a Cherokee breed. He's mostly white, but he's a citizen of the Cherokee Nation. He's also a Confederate."

"Are we in the Cherokee Nation already?" Ben said.

"No. We're still in Arkansas. Boyd built his house just across the line."

He pointed to some hills beyond the house. "Just over there," he said. "That's the Cherokee Nation. If we ride a couple of old Boyd's horses, we'll be there before you know it."

"It'll sure feel good to be on a horse," Ben said. "My feet are killing me."

"We'll have to wait until dark," said Dhu.

"Has he got any dogs down there?" Ben asked.

"I don't know," said Dhu. "If there are any, we'll toss them some of Elder Coon's jerky, see if that quiets them down any. If that doesn't work, well, we'll just have to deal with the problem when the time comes. If we're lucky, there won't be any menfolk around. They ought to be off with Stand Watie somewhere. Might be a slave or two around, though."

"Indians own slaves?" said Ben.

"Some do."

"You?"

"No. I don't believe in owning people. None of the Pins do."

They eased themselves back down the hill a little way and rolled over on their backs to relax and wait for the sun to go down. It had been a long walk, and they were weary. Dhu slept first, and Ben realized that he felt very lonely and vulnerable without Dhu watching and making decisions. He didn't like the feeling. It meant that he was dependent on the Indian, that he needed him. Ben didn't want to need Dhu Walker. In fact, he told himself, Dhu Walker was the last person on earth he would want to need, except maybe Old Harm. He forced his mind to focus again on the horses, and he crawled back up to the top of the hill. Maybe he would see some movement down there and learn something about who was around and what they were doing. He saw a dog. "Damn," he muttered to himself. Well, as Dhu had said, they would just have to deal with the problem.

A noise from behind startled Ben, and he turned quickly — too quickly, he thought.

"See anything?" said Dhu, moving up beside him.

"A dog," Ben said.

"Well, at least we know. Why don't you try to grab some sleep? I'll watch up here awhile."

Ben rolled over on his back and closed his eyes. He was just humoring Dhu, he told himself; he would rest his eyes for a few minutes. Soon he was sound asleep, and when Dhu shook him by the arm, it was dark. He sat up quickly.

"Take it easy," Dhu said.

"I — I must have gone to sleep," said Ben.

"Yeah. Get up and walk around a little."

Ben stood and stretched, then paced down the hill and back up.

"I'm ready," he said. "You see anything more while I was asleep?"

"One old black man," Dhu said. "He

came out the back door and pitched some water. There's no way to tell how many people are in that house or who they might be. Well, let's go."

From down below they heard just then the deep baying of a hunting dog.

"What's that sound like to you?" Dhu said.

"That old dog has jumped a rabbit."

"Right. We're in luck. Let's move fast."

They ran down the hill and around to the back of the barn. They could still hear the deep voice of the hound in the distance. They circled around to the front of the barn and lifted off the rails that served as a corral gate. They saddled two horses, a chestnut mare and a peppery gray gelding. Ben mounted the mare, and Dhu handed him the reins to the gelding.

"Hold him," he said. He drove the other horses through the gate and out of the corral. Then he ran back to where Ben waited and vaulted into the saddle on the gelding. "Let's go," he said, and they were racing toward the Cherokee Nation.

The next evening Dhu and Ben rode up to a small log cabin deep in the woods. Dhu held up a hand, and they halted. Ben started to swing down out of the saddle.

"Hold it," said Dhu. "Just wait."

Ben gave him a curious look. Presumably this was their destination. Why, then, he wondered, did Dhu not just climb down and knock on the door? Why sit here and wait? Wait for what? The door of the cabin opened just a crack. Then it opened a little wider and a face appeared from within. It was the face of an Indian in his mid-fifties, a small man. The door opened farther and the man spoke.

"Gago hia?" he said. "Inoli?"

"Yes," said Dhu. "It is. Speak English, Ready. I have a friend with me. He doesn't know Cherokee."

"Get down," said Ready. "Come in."

Dhu climbed down out of the saddle. "Come on, Ben," he said. Ready walked out to greet them just as Ben got to the ground. "This is Ben Lacey. He's a Yankee soldier from Iowa."

"Hello," said Ready, extending his hand to Ben. Ben took it and was surprised at the gentleness of the man's grip. "My name is Ready Ballard. You're welcome here."

"Thank you," said Ben.

Ready turned to Dhu and shook his hand.

"I'm glad to see you," he said. "I heard

they took you into Arkansas to fight."

"I was arrested by the Confederates," Dhu said. "They thought I had turned on them."

"Did you?"

"Maybe just a little. Anyhow, that's how I met Ben. He was a prisoner, too. We escaped together."

"Well, you're both welcome here," said Ready. "Go in the house. It's all right. I'm alone here. I'll take care of your horses."

They went inside while Ready Ballard unsaddled the horses, corraled them, and fed them. Soon he joined them inside and served fresh-caught catfish and corn bread and wild greens. The three of them talked long into the night and drank strong black coffee boiled in a pot over the fire. Ben was astonished at this man, the second Indian he had ever met. Ready Ballard was a fullblood Cherokee, and yet his English was every bit as good as Dhu's — and Dhu's was better than his own Iowa farm English, though Ben hated to admit that, even to himself. In the course of the evening, Ben learned that the Cherokee Nation operated its own school system, which was temporarily shut down because of the war, and that Ready Ballard was a teacher. He had been Dhu's teacher before Dhu went away to college. Ben had his own notion of what Indians were like, and he was struggling to hold on to that notion; these two men did not fit the image in his mind.

Ben had not yet decided to like Dhu Walker. He had not yet accepted the idea of the Pin Indians being forced to become rebels and then turning on other rebels during the battle. And then there were those stories he'd heard about the Indians taking scalps during the battle. He had been forced into a temporary companionship with Dhu, but he wasn't at all sure he liked the man. Ready Ballard, on the other hand, was a generous and kind host. Ben couldn't remember ever having met a nicer gentleman, but he remained suspicious. The man, after all, was an Indian. Indians were savages. They were not to be trusted. Ben was confused.

When Ben woke up late the following morning, he found that Dhu was up ahead of him and Ready had gone somewhere to find them some clothes. He and Dhu made coffee and ate some breakfast. They had just finished when Ready returned with their clothes. Dhu and Ben bathed and nursed their scratches, bruises, and sore feet.

The clothes Ready had procured were not new, but they were in good condition.

Each had a pair of tall, black boots, which pretty nearly fit. Dhu had a three-piece black suit and a white shirt. He put on the trousers, shirt, and vest and tucked the trouser legs into the tall boots. Ben's new trousers were gray. He also had a black suit coat and vest.

"Thanks a lot, Ready," said Dhu, feeling better, now that he was cleaned up and wearing new clothes. "We sure do appreciate it."

"Yeah," Ben said. "Thanks."

"I'm glad to help, boys," said Ready. "You're welcome to stay here as long as you like. It's a pretty good place to hide out. Nobody much comes up here."

"We'll stay tonight and then head out early in the morning," said Dhu. "We've got a job to do."

"Can you tell me about it?"

"The rebels have got a gold shipment coming up from Mexico," Dhu told him. "We're going to intercept it."

"A gold shipment ought to have a pretty good guard on it," said Ready.

"Yeah. We'll need to get some guns. And we could use some help, if any is available."

"You know Middle Striker?" Ready said.

"Sure."

"The Confederates didn't get him and his friends. They're all holed up at Middle Striker's place. You know where he lives?"

"I've been there," Dhu said. "Do you know who's with him?"

"Hair, Bird-in-Close, Bear-at-Home, Ketch Barnett. Last I knew."

"We'll go check them out," Dhu said.

"Old Harm's already got a head start on us," said Ben. "We fool around much longer, he'll be way ahead of us."

"That's all right," said Dhu. "We don't need to catch him on his way down, and we know which road he's taking on the way back. That's our advantage. We've got time."

"Old Harm?" said Ready. "You boys fixing to tackle Gordon Early?"

Ben glanced at Dhu, then looked back at Ready. "You heard of him?" he asked.

"Just about everyone around here has," Ready said. "He's a tough one. And mean. You be careful."

He walked across the room, opened a drawer, and took out of it something wrapped in an old cloth. He placed the bundle on the table and unfolded the cloth to reveal a Model 1851 Navy Colt, a flask of powder, some lead balls, and a tin of caps.

"This is all I've got," he said. "Take it."

Dhu picked up the Colt and tucked it into the waistband of Ben's trousers. Ben looked at Dhu, surprised, but Dhu pretended not to notice. Ben picked up the flask, balls, and caps and dropped them into his vest pockets. He looked at Ready.

"Thanks again," he said.

The next morning they were up and dressed early. Ready Ballard fed them a big breakfast. While they ate, he saddled their horses and led them around to the front of the house. Then he joined Ben and Dhu for one last cup of coffee.

Ben loaded the Colt. They had nothing to pack, no extra clothes except their jackets, and they were soon off, headed deeper into the woods, farther into the Cherokee Nation. Once again Ben had that uneasy feeling. He had been with two Indians. He was about to find himself alone with six of them. He had no clear idea where he was; he just figured he was somewhere west of Arkansas.

8

Ben was nervous at Middle Striker's house. He was more than nervous; he was scared. He tried not to let it show, but he stayed close to Dhu at all times. There were five full-blooded Indian men and three women there when Dhu and Ben arrived. Of the full-bloods, only Ketch Barnett could speak English.

The first night he slept there, after having ridden almost all day from Ready Ballard's place, Ben had visions of being tortured, killed, and scalped. He wondered if the whole trip had been a ruse of Dhu's for getting a white captive into the clutches of this band of savages. His imagination was lively, and it filled his sleep that night with dreams.

Naturally, Dhu talked Cherokee to the others, and Ben thought they were talking about him, especially when they laughed. Dhu would speak to him now and then in English and supposedly tell him what they had been talking about, and Ketch Barnett tried a time or two to engage Ben in conversation, but Ben was not very talkative.

In his more rational moments, he realized that his isolation was at least as much his own fault as that of the Cherokees. In fact, he noted to himself, he was probably being downright surly. He thought he should do something to change that impression, but he didn't know how to go about it, and he couldn't quite bring himself to make the effort.

The food was certainly good, and there was plenty of it. Ben couldn't complain about that. He did have a time remembering the names and putting the right name to each man.

Middle Striker, in whose home they were gathered, was a man of medium height with a hard, slender body. His black hair, which showed a few streaks of premature gray, was cropped just below the ears and hung down over his forehead to just above his heavy eyebrows. His eyes were so dark they looked black, and his skin had the hue of polished mahogany. He wore only trousers, smoked a corncob pipe, and kept an old Remington six-gun handy and loaded at all times. He spoke only Cherokee.

Hair was even darker than Middle Striker and maybe three inches shorter, but he was stocky and probably outweighed Middle Striker by ten or fifteen pounds. His shiny black hair was cut short. His eyes were small and set close together, and they seemed to bore into Ben when Hair gave him a direct look. Hair looked to him like a man who had never smiled. He wore white man's clothes, except for a long red sash that was wrapped several times around his waist, the loose ends hanging free to below his left knee. A long, wide-bladed hunting knife was tucked into the sash. Hair spoke only Cherokee.

Bird-in-Close was aptly named. He was small, wiry, and angular. He had a beaklike nose, thin lips, big round eyes, and a habit of sitting with his knees drawn up to his chest and his arms wrapped around them. He, too, was dark. He knew a few words of English.

Also appropriately named, Ben thought, was Bear-at-Home. Over six feet tall and weighing at least two hundred fifty pounds, he wore a listless expression, ate constantly, and perspired heavily. He was not quite as dark as the others. Ben assumed that Bear did not speak English, although he never heard Bear say anything at all.

Ketch Barnett, the one English speaker, was the tallest, standing well over six feet. A handsome fellow with a fetching smile, he had a slender, athletic build and an easy manner. Ben thought Ketch was the friendliest of the bunch, but he realized that was only because Ketch could speak English.

The three women, Ben found out, were the wives of Ketch, Bear, and Middle Striker. Their children were staying at Hair's home with his wife and some other women.

Ben and Dhu spent a second night at Middle Striker's house and ate breakfast there the next morning. The men all sat around the table and talked Cherokee. Ben felt uneasy and left out. He could tell from their facial expressions and the tone of their voices that the conversation was serious. He poured himself another cup of coffee, just so he would have something to do. After a while, there was a pause, and Dhu looked at Ben.

"I've told them about our plan, Ben," he said, "and they're going to help us. All of them. You and me are going to ride south on the Texas Road until we encounter Old Harm. We'll see how many men are with him. We'll ride back and find a good spot on the trail to make our play, and we'll estimate the time it will take him to get to that spot. Then one of us will ride back up here to tell the others."

Ben nodded. He wondered if he would be the one who would have to come back after the full-bloods. He hoped not. He didn't want to venture into this territory alone. He decided to keep that sentiment to himself for the time being. Once they had located Old Harm, if Dhu told him to ride back up here, he'd just refuse to do it.

"Does that sound all right to you?" Dhu said.

"Yeah. Sounds fine. We sure will need the help."

"You'll also need some supplies and some more weapons," said Ketch. "We'll take care of that, too, before you leave."

"When do we go?" Ben asked.

"First thing in the morning," said Dhu.

They were up before the sun with blanket rolls containing extra clothing tied behind their saddles. A rifle was strapped to each horse, and Ben and Dhu each carried a six-gun and had another stowed in the saddlebags, along with extra ammunition. They also had plenty of trail food, and Dhu carried a spyglass. The Pins had supplied them well.

Ben was glad to be on the trail once more. He was well rested and well fed. Of course, he was apprehensive about the attack on Old Harm and his troops, but the actual encounter was still remote, still unreal in his mind, and when he tried to force himself to think realistically about it, he simply told himself that he was in no more danger than if he had not been captured in the first place, but rather still had battles to face with the cannon crew. He was probably in even less danger than he would have been had he remained a prisoner. He would just take this latest adventure one step at a time, and he told himself he could actually back out of this whole thing at any time, if he should decide to.

They did not talk much as they rode south. Dhu thought of his companion as a surly, ignorant farm boy. He was also a white man, *ayonega,* and white men were responsible for all the miseries of the Cherokees — well, most of the really big ones, anyway. For the time being he needed Ben, but he talked to him only when it was necessary — to say they needed to rest the horses, or they would camp here for the night, or they needed to turn this way or that. Nothing more.

Ben, on the other hand, could not rid himself of his notion of the savage redskin. He had seen too many pictures on the covers of cheap storybooks showing a naked savage wielding a war club over the head of an innocent, cowering white woman. He had heard too many lurid tales of torture and massacre. It was true that Dhu and his friends, especially Ready Ballard and Ketch Barnett, did not really fit that image, and that caused some confusion and conflict in Ben's mind, but the old notion was persistent. It had been deeply ingrained in Ben during his boyhood.

They had ridden most of the day away, but the sun was not yet down when Dhu pointed off to his left toward a river flowing almost parallel to the road.

"We've got to stop here," he said.

"It's early yet," said Ben, but he followed Dhu off the road and down to the riverbank.

"The town of Tahlequah's just ahead," said Dhu, dismounting and starting to unsaddle his horse. "It could be full of Confederate troops. No sense in taking chances."

"Is there a way around the town?"

"Not hardly. It's best to wait and go through after dark. We'll stop for the night somewhere on the other side of town."

They unsaddled both horses and let them drink from the river, then allowed them to graze freely along the bank. Ben and Dhu ate sparingly from the rations the Pins had prepared for them.

"What did you call that town up ahead?" said Ben.

"Tahlequah."

"That's an Indian name?"

"It's a Cherokee name," said Dhu. "It's our capital city."

Ben thought it sounded strange for an Indian to talk about his capital city. He thought Indians lived in villages, which they moved around from time to time. He began to be really curious about this place called Tahlequah.

"What's it mean?" he said.

"What?"

"The name of that town up ahead."

"Tahlequah?"

"Yeah," said Ben. "Tahlequah. What's it mean?"

"It means Mussel Shell Place," said Dhu. "The Cherokee word for 'mussel' actually means 'it has two sides' — you know, like a mussel shell. And 'Tahlequah' means 'the place where you find mussels.' "

"And it's your capital city?"

"Yeah."

"The capital city of the Cherokee Nation?"

"That's right. But it's been captured by the Cherokee Confederates. That's why I wound up in that damn battle with all those rebels. We're going to have to be real quiet when we sneak through that town."

Dhu folded his hands behind his head and lay back in the grass. Under the trees a short distance away, snowbirds fussed around on the ground. Now and then they flew short distances, only to light again and fuss some more.

Ben sat staring at the ground before him. "It's a damn shame," he said.

"What's that?"

"A man having to sneak through his own capital city like that."

Dhu looked up at Ben expecting to see something of a smirk on the Iowan's face, but the expression there was serious, almost sad. He was surprised at that expression of sympathy. He lowered his head again and stared up at the sky. It wouldn't be long before the sun went down.

"Yeah," he said. "It is a damn shame."

Tahlequah was quiet and dark when they rode in. Ben was struck by how much it looked like any other small town in the country. He wasn't at all sure what he had expected, but he hadn't thought that an Indian town, especially a capital city, would look just, well, ordinary. But it did. He was thinking they might get through the town with no problems when a rider carrying a rifle slipped out of the shadows.

"Hold it right there," he said.

"What's the trouble?" Dhu asked.

"Dhu Walker?" said the rider. "Is that you?"

"Hello, Charlie. Just passing through."

"Who's that with you?"

"Just a friend."

"There's another guard at the other end of town," said Charlie. "He likes to go by the book."

"Thanks, Charlie," said Dhu. "We'll be careful."

Dhu urged his horse forward and Ben followed. They had only gone a few paces when Charlie spoke again.

"Dhu?" he said.

Dhu and Ben stopped their horses.

Charlie rode up beside them. "Go down about to the government buildings," he said. "Wait till you hear a racket down here. That other guard will come riding hard to see what's wrong. When he passes you by, you can go on out of town."

"*Wado,*" said Dhu. "Thanks, friend."

Ben touched the brim of his hat and

nodded, then followed Dhu down the road to a spot where three small buildings stood on one end of a large, tree-filled square. Dhu led Ben into the trees. They had waited no more than a minute when they heard three shots from the direction from which they had ridden into town. Ben jumped at the sound.

"Charlie," said Dhu.

They waited impatiently and tense there in the dark until a rider came from the south.

"Get ready," Dhu said.

The rider raced past them. Dhu let him go on out of sight. Then he motioned Ben to follow and kicked his horse into a gallop.

Dhu rode hard across the square and back out onto the road, with Ben right behind him. They kept up the pace until they had left Tahlequah a fair distance behind them. Then they slowed their mounts to a walk.

"What was that all about back there?" Ben asked.

"Confederate guards," Dhu said.

"Why'd that first one help us?"

"He's an old friend," said Dhu. "Sometimes that still comes first."

They rode another mile or so down the

road before Dhu called a halt. He led Ben off to the left side of the road.

"We'll stop here," he said.

"For the night?"

"Yeah."

They started preparing to spend the night in a basic camp with no fire.

"What will we run into next?" said Ben.

"Fort Gibson's our next big obstacle," said Dhu. "Right now I don't even know which side has got it."

9

Another five days of riding carried Dhu and Ben into the Chickasaw Nation in the southern part of what the United States government had begun calling Indian Territory. They passed Fort Gibson with no problems. Seeing it occupied, but still unable to determine by which side it was occupied, Dhu led Ben in a wide arc around the fort. It really didn't matter who was in there; they didn't have an explanation to offer either side. The rest of the trail south on the Texas Road, which they picked up just south of Fort Gibson, was dull and boring. They spotted one mounted patrol — Dhu thought it was Confederate, but he wasn't sure — and managed to avoid being seen by it. They were almost to Texas before their food supply began to run low.

"One more day," said Dhu, "and we'll cross the Red River."

"And then we'll be in Texas?" Ben said.

"That's right."

"That's one place I never thought I'd see."

Dhu had a sudden uneasy feeling. He

kept riding, but his eyes were searching the landscape around them. "If we're not careful," he said, "we may not either one of us see it yet."

"What?" Ben had picked up on Dhu's sudden alertness. "What is it?"

A rifle shot rang out, and a bullet kicked up dust in the road just between the two horses.

"Take cover," Dhu shouted. He grabbed his rifle, flung himself from the saddle, and rolled toward the edge of the road. Ben was a little slower, but he imitated Dhu's actions and rolled to the opposite side of the road. Another rifle shot rang out. The nervous and riderless horses trotted on up the road, carrying with them what was left of the supplies, including the extra handguns and ammunition.

"Where are they?" said Ben. "Did you see anyone?"

Dhu raised his head a little to look down the road. Large boulders lined both sides of the road, and low mountains rose sharply to the east. Not far ahead a sharp ridge overlooked the road.

"No," said Dhu, "but there's only one place they can be. See that ridge up ahead?"

Ben peered out from around the edge of

a boulder on the other side of the road. "I see it," he said.

Just then a figure raised itself up on top of the ridge. Dhu and Ben could see the silhouette of a man with a rifle. The man stepped to the edge of the ridge.

"You down there," he shouted. "Who are you?"

"Who wants to know?" said Dhu.

"Soldiers of the Choctaw Nation in the service of the Confederacy. Identify yourselves."

"Travelers," answered Dhu. "Just passing through. Going to Texas."

"Dhu," Ben said in a loud whisper, "what are we going to do?"

Before Dhu could answer, the rebel on the ridge was shouting again.

"Come out in the road with your hands up. Both of you. We'll decide whether you pass through or not."

Dhu made a quick decision. He stood up and propped his rifle on the top of the boulder, taking aim at the exposed rebel. He squeezed off a round. There seemed to be too much time between the pop of the rifle and the shout from the man on the ridge. Then the dark figure fell backward. Again there was a pause. Three more men appeared on the ridge and began firing.

Dhu ducked back behind his boulder. He could hear the bullets smashing into the rock above his head. Ben huddled down behind his own protective cover, but he soon realized that all the shots were aimed at Dhu. He took a deep breath, stood up, aimed, and fired. On the ridge another rebel fell back. Ben dropped back down out of sight.

"Did you get him?" said Dhu.

"I got him."

"I think there are only two more up there," said Dhu.

"That's all I made out."

There was silence while both sides reloaded their rifles.

"It looks like a standoff," said Ben.

"It looks that way," Dhu said. "Here. Take this."

Ben looked up in time to catch the rifle that Dhu tossed across the road to him.

"What are you going to do?" he said.

"While you keep them busy," Dhu said, "I'm going to try to get up there and around behind them."

Ben raised himself up, but he didn't see anybody on the ridge. He dropped back down and turned to look at Dhu, who was already trotting up the road in the direction from which they had come. Ben started to call out to him, but stopped himself. Dhu disappeared behind some more boulders.

"I just hope he makes it," said Ben to himself. He raised his head to take another look, and a figure on the ridge fired a shot. Ben dropped down just in time. He felt a shower of rock particles as the bullet struck the boulder just above his head. He stood up with his rifle ready, but the shooter had dropped back to safety. He waited, ready to fire. Another rebel appeared, but Ben had to swing his rifle to his right to take aim. Both men fired at almost the same time. Both missed. Both ducked back to safety. Ben set aside the rifle that Dhu had tossed him and picked up his own. All was quiet. He put it down again and reloaded the first one. Where the hell was Dhu?

Dhu ran about a hundred yards back up the road before starting to climb. It didn't take him long to reach the top of the hill where he stopped to take a quick look around. He could see no one. Then he heard a shot. He ran down the far side of the hill and started moving south. Somewhere along the way he would find a back path up to the ridge the rebels were on. He heard two more shots. He hoped the last shot had not hit Ben. Then he saw four horses hobbled just ahead. Again he looked around. The hill rose sharply just above the horses. That had to be the spot the men were shooting from, just up there.

Dhu moved slowly and carefully up to the horses. They were saddled, but not with military-issue saddles. Most of the rebels Dhu had run into had been forced to supply themselves, though, so that didn't prove anything one way or the other. For that matter, most of the Union soldiers in the Indian Territory had to furnish their own supplies. You couldn't always tell one from the other.

Dhu pulled the pistol out of his belt, checked it, and started up the hill. He heard another shot; it sounded as if it had come from the hilltop up above. That was good. That meant they were still shooting at Ben. They hadn't hit him yet, unless that last shot had been the one. There was another shot. This one sounded farther off. Ben was shooting back.

Dhu came to a level spot on the back of the hill, and there he found a body. One of the two they had hit, he thought. The man had fallen back and rolled down the hill to this level spot. There was a neat hole in the man's forehead. A lucky shot, Dhu thought. He pulled the pistol out of the man's belt and tucked it in his own. He leaned forward, partly to balance his weight while climbing uphill, partly to avoid being seen by the men on the ridge and to maintain a low profile when they started shooting. Up a little higher he saw the second body off to his right lying in a grotesquely contorted position. He gave it only a cursory glance. Like the first one, it had the appearance of a white man. He was glad.

He heard another shot from a distance. Ben's shot. Then he heard one from above. Then he saw them. The man who had just fired had dropped back down and turned to reload, and he saw Dhu coming. But the other man was standing up and aiming a shot at Ben. Dhu thought fast. He raised his pistol and fired, and the man who was aiming his rifle jerked, groaned, and toppled forward. The other man tossed aside his rifle and groped for a six-gun in his belt. Dhu cocked his six-gun and swung it around toward the remaining rebel, but the man rolled to his right, and Dhu's shot kicked up dirt. The rebel fired just as Dhu dropped to the ground, and the shot went harmlessly over his head. Dhu stretched his arm out before him and fired again. He heard the man expel his breath loudly as if he had been kicked in the chest, and he saw a bright red pool begin to form and spread on the man's sternum. The man stared at his own chest for a moment, his eyes wide. Then he fell back and lay still.

Dhu ran to each of the three bodies on the hill, picking up the guns. The fourth had fallen off the front of the ridge. He went up close to the edge and called out to Ben.

"Ben," he shouted. "You all right?"

"Yeah," came Ben's answer.

"It's over," said Dhu. "I'll be right down."

Carrying the extra guns, Dhu trotted down to the rebels' horses. He took off their hobbles, gathered up the reins of three horses, and mounted the fourth. Then he rode back the way he had come, leading the three extra horses. Soon he was back on the road. Ben was standing in the middle of the road waiting when Dhu rode up.

"Look what we got," said Dhu.

"Not bad," said Ben. He picked a horse and mounted up, and they rode down to where the fourth rebel's body lay face down in the road. Dhu got off his horse and rolled the body over with his foot. There was a pistol in the man's belt. He took it. He didn't see the rifle, and he didn't want to take the time to search for it. They were pretty well armed without it anyhow. They had the four pistols and two rifles they had been given by the Pins, and now they had four more pistols and three more rifles. They had lost their own horses and supplies, but they had picked up four saddled horses. All four carried saddle rolls and saddlebags. They would check to see what kinds of supplies they carried later on down the road.

"Let's go," he said.

Two miles down the road, they found their own horses and caught them without much trouble. Dhu looked around. To the west was a wide flat prairie. At the far edge of the prairie was a row of trees.

"I'll bet there's a creek back there," he said. "Let's check it out."

There was a creek, and they made camp. They even risked a small fire. They used the last of their rations to cook themselves a hot meal of beans and pork, and they boiled some coffee. After they had eaten, they checked the saddlebags on the rebels' horses. They found food, coffee, and ammunition. They staked the horses for the night, then rolled out their own blankets.

In the morning they were up with the sun. They made a quick breakfast, drank some coffee, and started to break camp. Dhu looked at the saddles.

"We going to leave the extra horses here?" Ben asked.

"No," said Dhu. "Let's saddle them up."

"We'll look kind of suspicious, won't we?" said Ben. "Leading four saddled horses?"

"Yeah," Dhu said. "But we've got to cross that river in a little while. You got any money?"

"No."

"Me neither. We can take the ferry or we can spend all day looking for a good crossing. It costs money to ride the ferry."

"You think we can trade off them saddles for a ride?"

"That's what I'm thinking," said Dhu. "If we're lucky, maybe we won't run into anybody else between here and there."

They saddled the horses, packed up all their goods, and left. In a few hours they came to the ferry, which was no more than a large raft with side rails. The vessel was lashed to a guy rope that was anchored on either side of the river. A sign was posted at the side of the road: Colbert's Ferry.

A tall, lanky man with dark hair stepped out from inside a canvas military tent. Ben took the man for an Indian. At least a half-breed, like Dhu, he thought.

"I'm Colbert," said the man.

"We want to cross over," Dhu said.

"You see the prices on the sign," said Colbert. "Ten cents for each man. Twenty-five cents for each horse. You got the fare?"

"Is that Yankee money," said Dhu, "or Confederate?"

"I ain't particular," said Colbert. "I'll take either one."

"Well, we don't have either one," Dhu said. "Would you take a saddle?"

Colbert walked over to inspect the four riderless horses. He gave Dhu a sideways look. "The worst of these is worth more than the cost of the ferry," he said.

"It all depends on your point of view," said Dhu. "We need to get across the river. We have no money. We have extra saddles. Is it a deal?"

"Which one?" Colbert said.

"Take your pick."

Colbert grabbed a saddle by the horn and gave it a tug.

"I'll take this one," he said.

"I'll unbuckle it for you." Dhu dismounted and unsaddled the other horse. "Can we leave the other saddles here with you?" he said.

"What for?"

"For safekeeping," said Dhu. "We'll be coming back this way. We may need to work another trade. Then again, there's always a chance we won't make it back at all. We don't come back, they're all yours."

"How long do I have to hold them?"

"Say thirty days."

"Deal," Colbert said.

Ben was still sitting on his horse, staring across the river. "That Texas over there?" he asked.

"Yeah," said Colbert. "That where you want to go?"

"Yeah," said Ben, still staring in near disbelief.

"Ben," said Dhu, "get down and help me unsaddle these brutes."

At Colbert's instruction, they put the four saddles inside the tent. They also took off the bridles and stored them. They tied lead ropes on the four riderless horses and loaded them on the ferry. Colbert ferried Dhu across with the four horses, then went back for Ben and the two remaining horses. As Ben led the two horses off the ferry and Colbert prepared to recross the river, Dhu stepped up to the raft.

"Have you taken any Confederate soldiers across lately?" he said.

Colbert gave him another sideways look. Then he shrugged. "About a week ago," he said. "One officer son of a bitch and eight more. Nine men and nine horses in all. When I asked for my money, the officer pulled a gun on me, made me take them across for free. Then he cut my rope and set me adrift. I damn near drowned saving my ferry. Took me two more days to get it back in operation."

"Thanks," said Dhu. He turned and headed up the bank toward the horses.

Colbert had started back across the river, but he shouted at Dhu just as he reached his mount. "Remember," he said, "thirty days. You don't show up by then, those saddles are mine."

Dhu waved at Colbert, then swung up into the saddle.

"That officer sounds like Old Harm to me," Ben said.

"It was him," said Dhu. "I'd bet on it."

"He's probably two hundred miles south of here by now."

"That's all right," said Dhu. "He'll be coming back on the same road."

10

They hadn't gone far into Texas before they emerged from the woods and looked over a vast rolling prairie. Here and there a lone tree or a small clump of trees dotted the otherwise monotonous landscape. Wide-eyed, Ben turned in his saddle, trying to take it all in. Looking east along the line of trees that crept up from the river, he saw a column of smoke curling up into the sky. He turned to face Dhu.

"I'd say that was coming from a chimney, wouldn't you?" he asked.

"Likely a farmhouse," Dhu said.

"I'm awful tired of your cooking." Ben smiled. "And mine."

"Well," said Dhu, "let's check it out."

They headed across the grassland toward the smoke, and as they topped a slight rise, they saw a road ahead. It wasn't much more than a couple of wagon tracks, but it looked as if it led to the farm. They decided to follow it. They had just turned onto the road when Dhu twisted around in the saddle and looked back.

"Ben," he said.

Ben looked over his shoulder and saw riders coming. There were eight or ten of them, and they were riding hard, straight toward Ben and Dhu.

"Come on." Dhu kicked the sides of his horse and headed for the trees. Ben kept right beside him, leading the four extra horses behind him.

"Have they seen us?" Dhu shouted to Ben.

"I don't know, but they're still coming," said Ben.

They reached the trees and slowed their pace, then pulled off to one side, taking cover in the woods. Neither man spoke, but almost simultaneously they drew their revolvers from their belts and held them ready. They waited a few tense minutes. They could hear the riders approaching. They watched the trail. The sound of pounding hooves came closer, and as it did, Ben and Dhu could hear voices, cursing and shouting. They thumbed back the hammers of their revolvers and waited. The riders came thundering down the road, through the woods, and past the place where Ben and Dhu were hiding. They were hurrying toward the farmhouse.

"What's going on?" Ben asked.

"I don't know. Let's find out." Dhu

swung down out of the saddle and took the lead ropes for the four extra horses. He tethered the horses to a tree, then got back up on his horse.

"Come on," he said.

They rode out onto the trail and followed the riders.

"Go easy," said Dhu.

The sound of the hoofbeats had ceased, but up ahead they could hear rough voices shouting. Dhu motioned toward the woods on the right side of the trail. Ben nodded and rode in among the trees. Dhu went off the trail to his left. They rode slowly through the trees until they came to the edge of the area that had been cleared to make room for the farmhouse. It was a neat, sturdy little house in a well-kept yard with several outbuildings and small corrals and pens. The house faced south with the river at its back. To the east stood a small barn. One of the riders was shouting toward the house. Ben and Dhu quietly dismounted and kept out of sight.

"McClellan. You and the boy come on out, and we'll leave the womenfolk be."

A woman's voice came from inside the house: "Sam Ed's only fourteen. Go away and leave us alone."

"That's old enough to make a soldier,"

said the rider. "Last chance, McClellan. Bring the boy out, or we'll figure you for a Yankee sympathizer."

The front door of the house opened, and a tall, rawboned man with a bushy mustache stepped out onto the porch. He was carrying a shotgun.

"There's no figuring to be done, Kilpatrick," he said. "It ain't no secret that I'm against this war. But I ain't bothering nobody. So you and your mob get off my land and leave us be. That's my last word."

"There's ten of us," Kilpatrick said. "You can't fight us all."

"Get out," said McClellan.

The man next to Kilpatrick reached for a six-gun. "That's it," he said, pulling the gun from its holster.

McClellan fired the shotgun and blasted the man from the saddle. Before the body hit the ground, McClellan stepped back inside and slammed the door. Nine riders began firing at the house. Finally Kilpatrick raised his arm and shouted.

"Hold it. Hold it," he said. "Stop shooting."

There were a couple of shots fired after that, but then they all stopped.

"McClellan," Kilpatrick yelled, "everyone in there will get killed if we keep this up. Come on out now and spare your family. We'll hang you and see that the boy gets conscripted, and then we'll leave your wife and daughter alone. Come out or we'll kill the bunch of you."

From behind a tree, Dhu raised his revolver and took careful aim. He squeezed the trigger, and his bullet tore into Kilpatrick's back just between the shoulder blades. Kilpatrick threw his arms up and screamed in pain and surprise. Then he slumped forward and lay lifeless over his horse's neck. Some of the riders turned around to look for the source of the shot. When they did, a rifle barrel came out a window of the house and fired. Another rider fell.

Dhu ran back farther into the trees, but he still had a clear shot at some of the riders in the yard. For an instant the riders fidgeted nervously, undecided whether to shoot into the woods or back at the house.

Ben shouted into the silence from his spot in the woods on the other side of the road. "We've got you surrounded," he said. "Throw down your guns and clear out."

A rider spun his horse in the direction of Ben's voice and raised his revolver. A shot from Ben's gun knocked the man out of the saddle. Another rider threw up his hands.

"All right. All right," he shouted. "Don't shoot." The other riders caught the mood and raised their hands.

"Throw your guns to the ground," said Ben.

The riders started dropping guns to the ground.

"Now pick up your friends and move out," Ben said.

After a moment's hesitation, some of the riders dismounted and loaded the bodies onto the backs of horses. Then they rode out the same way they had come in. When the riders had gone far enough down the trail, Ben and Dhu emerged from the woods. McClellan stepped out the front door and walked across the lawn to meet them. He held out his right hand.

"Thanks, whoever you are," he said. "I'm Herd McClellan."

"Mr. McClellan, I'm Dhu Walker, and this is my friend Ben Lacey."

"We were on our way up your trail in hopes you could spare some home-cooked food," Ben said.

"It's lucky for me you came along," McClellan said. "Come in the house and we'll do something about that meal."

They followed McClellan into the house. An older woman, a young woman, and a boy were standing in the room. The boy was still holding a rifle.

"You can put that away, Sam Ed," said McClellan. "These are friends. The others are gone — for now."

The boy walked across the room and hung the rifle on two pegs in the wall.

"This is my wife, Maude," said McClellan, "my daughter, Mary Beth, and that cautious youngster over there is my son, Sam Ed. Maude, children, these two young men just saved our lives. This is Dhu Walker and this is Ben Lacey. They're hungry, Maude."

Maude McClellan fixed a meal for which she apologized profusely. "If I'da knowed you was coming," she said, "I could have done a heap better."

Dhu and Ben assured her that the food was much better than what they were used to. Following the meal, they sat around the table with coffee.

"I couldn't help overhearing some of what was said out there," said Dhu. "Those men attacked you because you're opposed to the war?"

"I've supported Sam Houston from the beginning," McClellan said. "He worked hard to get Texas into the Union, and he tried like hell to keep it from pulling right back out again. He fought this damned secession all the way, and so did I. Well, we lost, but I'll be damned if I'll work for the rebels — or let my boy fight for them."

"Are there others around who think the way you do?" asked Ben.

"If there are, I ain't heard of them."

"Then all of your neighbors are your enemies?" Dhu said.

"It's their doing. Not mine."

"You'd all be safer somewhere else," Ben said. "Why don't you leave here?"

"And go where? This is my home, and nobody's going to run me out of it. Especially not any damn rebels."

"Herd," said Maude, "watch your language."

"You've got to get to safety," Ben said. "You said it yourself, I heard you. They'll be back."

"And if we ran off," McClellan said, "where would we go? We're surrounded by rebels. They'd get us for sure. No, sir. If we've got to fight rebels, we'll do it from right here."

Dhu drank the last of his coffee and set the cup down on the table. "Well," he said, "maybe you're right. We just came through

Indian Territory all the way from the Cherokee Nation, and we ran into a few rebel patrols on the way."

"You see?" said McClellan. "By the way, if you don't mind me asking, what are you boys up to?" He looked at Ben. "You've got the sound of a Yankee to me. No offense."

"I'm from Iowa," Ben said.

Dhu looked at Ben for a moment. Then he looked into the empty cup there before him. "Me and Ben," he said, "escaped from a troop of rebels. They captured us up in Arkansas. While we were prisoners Ben heard them talking about a gold shipment for the Confederacy coming into Mexico. A rebel captain named Early has been sent to pick it up and bring it back along the Texas Road. We're going to stop him."

"You boys are Yankee soldiers?" said McClellan.

"I am," Ben said. "First Iowa Battery."

"I was with the Cherokee Nation's home guard," said Dhu. "We were trying to keep the Confederacy out of the Cherokee Nation, since the United States refused to help us stay neutral. The rebels forced our chief to sign a treaty, and they put us in the rebel army. I ran off and got caught."

"I see," said McClellan.

"Dhu and I got caught by the same rebs," Ben said, "and then later we escaped together. Dhu, he led me down here."

McClellan looked at Dhu for a moment. "You a Cherokee?" he said.

"Yes," said Dhu. "Does it matter?"

"Nope," McClellan said. "What matters to me is that you ain't a damn rebel. I thought you had a Indian look about you. Cherokee, huh? Sam Houston lived with Cherokees. Good people."

Dhu stood up from the table. "Mr. McClellan," he said, "we left some horses out in the woods that we need to take care of."

"Call me Herd," said McClellan, "and I'll help you fetch them in. Come on, Sam Ed."

Ben got up from his chair and almost ran into Mary Beth, who had been standing quietly behind him listening to the conversation.

"Oh," she said.

"I'm sorry, miss," said Ben. "I'm a clumsy fool. I didn't even look where I was going."

Mary Beth blushed slightly and ducked her head, but she was smiling. "It was my fault," she said.

Ben looked at her for an awkward moment. She was real pretty, he thought. No, she was beautiful. He had never seen anyone so beautiful.

"No," he said, "it couldn't have been your fault. Excuse me."

He followed Dhu and McClellan out the front door. When he caught up with them, they were in the middle of a conversation.

"So what are your plans?" McClellan asked.

"They're not completely formulated, Herd," said Dhu. "We're going to ride on down the Texas Road until we spot Old Harm — that's what Early is called. When we spot him, we'll ride back up to the Cherokee Nation to get some of my friends to help us lay an ambush. That's pretty general yet, but that's it."

"You know he's coming on the Texas Road?"

"That's what I heard them say," Ben said.

"And he's got to go all the way to Mexico and then come back?"

"That's right," said Dhu.

"Well, you've got time on your side. You haven't determined your ambush spot yet?"

"No."

"You still need to do some planning, don't you?" McClellan said. "Why don't you use my place as your headquarters?"

"We don't want to be in your way," Dhu said.

"Nonsense. You need a place to stay. A place to work from, plan from. I owe you a favor, and besides, I believe in the same cause you do. I'd take it kindly if you'd accept my offer."

"All right," Dhu said. "We will."

"Good," said McClellan. "It's settled."

Dhu pointed up ahead into the trees. "Just there," he said.

They collected the four horses and headed back toward the house.

Ben thought about Mary Beth, and he was glad Dhu had accepted Herd McClellan's offer. Besides, he thought, the McClellans would need some help fighting off their neighbors. Those rebels would be back. McClellan had said it, Dhu had said it, and Ben knew they were right.

11

"Having all those horses in the corral sure looks good," said McClellan. "Raising horses has always been my desire. So far all I can afford to raise is corn and kids. Can't even afford to raise Cain no more."

There was work to be done on the corral and the barn that McClellan hadn't had time to do, and Ben and Dhu pitched in. Ben especially took to the work. Dhu wasn't sure if it was because Ben was just naturally a farmer or because he was so taken with Mary Beth. They stayed at the McClellan place for several days, killing time, just giving Old Harm time to come closer with the gold.

Ben, without shirking any chores, sought out every opportunity to talk to Mary Beth. Now and then he thought about his parents back on the farm in Iowa, and occasionally Old Harm and the gold invaded his mind, but mostly Ben lived contentedly in the present, his thoughts on Mary Beth and on the McClellan place.

Ben's contentment, however, was rudely

interrupted by Dhu one evening after supper.

"It's time we got down to business, Ben," he said. "One of us has got to go on down the trail and see if Old Harm is on his way back."

"What's the other'n going to do?" said Ben.

Dhu looked at Ben and saw the anxiety in his young face. He knew what was going on in the farm boy's mind. He smiled to himself, but outwardly he maintained a serious expression.

"Well," he said, "this is our headquarters. Someone'll have to stay here and protect it. Keep our supplies and horses in good shape. All that. I'm not much good at that kind of work, so, uh, I guess it'll have to be you."

Ben looked solemn. "Okay," he said.

Sitting across the table, Mary Beth smiled. She was not as concerned with appearances as were Ben and Dhu.

"When you find this Harm fella," said McClellan, "then what? You got to lay a trap, right? You got to get your friends, right? You got that all worked out?"

"Not exactly," Dhu said, "but I figure that when I locate Old Harm and his escort, I'll watch him long enough to make sure he is coming on this way. I figure he'll go right back to Colbert's ferry, the way he came down, and then back up the Texas Road to Fort Gibson. As soon as I've determined his movements, I'll come back here and get Ben. Then we'll ride up to get my friends in the Cherokee Nation. Old Harm will be moving north, and we'll be moving south along the same road. One of us will scout out ahead. As soon as we spot him coming, we'll lay the trap."

McClellan rubbed the stubble on his chin.

"I guess that's all right," he said. "It ain't my business nohow. But I think you'd do better to lay the trap where you want it, not wherever you happen to run acrost him."

"You're probably right about that," Dhu said, "but I don't know how I could work out the timing. I have to go back north to get my friends. Ben and I can make better time than those rebels can. They'll be hauling a heavy load of gold. If I lay an ambush too far south, maybe I won't get back with my friends in time. I don't see any other way to work it."

"You could go north right now," said McClellan. "Bring those men down here. That's what a headquarters is for, ain't it?

While you're fetching your friends, Ben could ride on south to scout out Old Harm."

Dhu looked thoughtful. He really wanted someone to stay with the McClellans in case their hostile neighbors came back, but there was a war going on.

"Yeah," he said. "With just a little bit of luck, we might all get back here at about the same time. We could let the rebels get almost to the river. They'd be out on the prairie, and we could be in the woods along the river waiting for them."

"Not bad," McClellan said, "but I've got an even better idea."

"Let's hear it," said Dhu.

"We mess up the ferry so they can't cross at Colbert's. They'd have to find another crossing. There's a place down here on my property where you can ford the river right now. It's kind of low. We steer them there, and we catch them right in the middle of the river. Catch them from both sides."

"We?" said Ben.

"We're going to help you on this," said McClellan. "Me and Sam Ed."

"Sam Ed's just a boy," Dhu said.

"Them Johnny Rebs want me in the army," Sam Ed protested.

"And who do you think fired that rifle

out the window and knocked that one fellow out of his saddle the other day?" said McClellan.

Dhu recalled the rifle shot, and he remembered seeing Sam Ed holding the rifle later. He thought about offering further arguments, but decided against it. War had a way of making men out of boys in a hurry, he thought. That was just one of the awful things it did. He let it go.

"All right," he said. "How do we guide Old Harm and his party to your ford? We can't just invite him on over to the ambush."

"Hell, I know that," McClellan said. "I may be just a dirt farmer, but I ain't stupid. He'll go to Colbert's ferry to cross. Right?"

"We think he will," Dhu said. "It makes sense."

"He'll find out that there ain't no ferry. Colbert or somebody will be there to holler acrost the river to him. He'll tell him there's a place down yonder where you can ford the river."

"It might work," said Dhu.

"Sounds good to me," Ben said.

"We'll start in the morning," Dhu said. "Right now I want to have a look at that ford."

"All right," said McClellan. "Let's go, then."

It was a good plan. Dhu had to admit it was better than his own. The river bottom was smooth at the ford but not too soft, and the banks were thick with big trees and heavy brush. There were two problems. One was the brush, which was too thick. McClellan said that he and Sam Ed would clear out a few select spots for the ambushers to hide in. They could do that while Ben and Dhu were out on the trail. The other problem was that Old Harm wouldn't be able to locate the spot. Beyond the thick woods was rolling grassland. There was no indication that anyone had been down to the river at that spot for a good long while — if ever. McClellan said that he and Sam Ed would create a trail. When they came to work on the brush, they would drive their wagon over to the Texas Road, across the prairie, and then down to the ford. They would make the trip enough times to blaze a trail to the ford. It would be a new trail, not much of a trail, but that would be all right. It would give the appearance that they wanted. It would seem as if the trail had been blazed because of the loss of the ferry.

* * *

The next morning Ben and Dhu rode out together. Each man carried two pistols and one rifle. They had left all the extra guns with the McClellans. All the guns were loaded and ready for use. The McClellans would have to stay alert and be prepared to drive off their overzealous neighbors if need be. Once out on the prairie, the two men rode together west to the Texas Road, where they parted company, Ben riding south and Dhu north.

Ben felt suddenly very much alone. He had left his parents' farm as a part of a military unit. At Elkhorn Tavern he had been captured by the rebels, and he had escaped with Dhu Walker. He had been with Dhu since then, and lately he had been with the McClellans. He had never been alone. Now he was riding alone in a strange country. Texas. What did he know about Texas? Nothing, except that it was filled with hostile rebels. He wondered what would happen if he had to talk to someone. Would they notice the way he talked? Would they know him right away for a Yankee? He decided that he would try to keep out of the way of people. But if he did get forced into the company of some Texans and they asked him questions, what would he say? Why was he not in the army? What was his business? Well, he thought, I'll just have to try to avoid that. And I'll have to be ready to shoot.

Riding along the trail he thought about Mary Beth. She had walked with him down the lane after supper. She had talked with him on the porch in the evenings. She smiled a lot when they were together. But that was all. He had not declared his feelings for her, though he realized the feelings were strong. He had not tried to kiss her, had not even held her hand. He wondered what she would have said if he had done so. He wondered what it would be like to kiss her, to — He tried to stop thinking in that direction. He knew he might not live through this war. But if he did, what then? Did he want to marry her? If he did, and if she would have him, what of his family? Would she go back to Iowa with him? Or would he stay in Texas and abandon his parents and his brothers and sisters?

And what would Herd think of all this? McClellan was grateful for Ben and Dhu's help in the fight and around the farm, and he was sympathetic to their cause, but how would he look on Ben as a prospective son-in-law? The old man might pick up his shotgun and run me off, he thought, and I guess I wouldn't blame him none.

Looking ahead on the road, he saw nothing, just a seemingly endless trail across nearly flat, dry grassland. Could anything really be at the end of that trail? How far did it go? And how long would he have to ride?

Dhu arrived at Colbert's ferry and was preparing to shout across the river to get Colbert's attention when the lanky ferryman appeared from behind his canvas tent.

"Hello," Colbert called.

"Hello. Can you ferry me across?"

"Coming right over."

When the raft arrived on the Texas side of the river, Dhu led his horse up on it, and Colbert began hauling them across.

"Another saddle for the ride?" Dhu said.

"That's too much," said Colbert. "I'll owe you another crossing."

"I'll be coming back with five friends and their horses."

"Another saddle will do it, then."

As he thought about McClellan's plan to disable Colbert's ferry, Dhu felt guilty. He wished there were some other way to get the job done, but he couldn't think of one. Well, they would compensate Colbert for his loss, one way or another. Dhu only hoped the ferryman would cooperate willingly, so that they wouldn't have to use any force. Back behind the tent Dhu could see where Colbert had begun building himself a house. It would be a shame to destroy what a man had put so much work into, to destroy a man's means of livelihood. He thought of the wanton destruction of property around Tahlequah and Park Hill, and then he thought about the many lost lives. It was the war. That was what war did. There was just no getting around it.

The raft touched the far shore, and Colbert secured it. Dhu led his horse onto the riverbank. He had a foot in the stirrup and was about to swing up into the saddle when four men seemed to materialize out of nowhere. They must have been hidden in the brush behind the tent, waiting. Each held a revolver in his hand. Dhu let his foot slip out of the stirrup. He stood looking across the saddle at the four men.

Colbert was still standing on the ferry. He, too, saw the men and stood still. "What's this about?" he said.

"We're taking over this ferry," said one of the four. Dhu took note of their appearance. They all looked like white men.

Their clothes were ragged and they were unshaven.

"For the Confederacy," said another. He had an evil leer on his face — his ugly face, thought Dhu.

"This ferry run is my business," said Colbert. "Authorized by the Chickasaw National Council."

"That's a Yankee council," said the first man. "That don't carry no weight no more. Walk away now or we'll blow you away."

One of the men took a step toward Dhu. "Who're you?" he said.

"Just a passenger," Dhu said. "Headed up to the Cherokee Nation."

"I seen that pistol in your belt," the man said. "Haul it up real easy, keepin' your elbow high, and pitch it over the saddle at me."

Dhu took hold of the butt of the six-gun in his belt, pulled it slowly upward, and tossed it over the horse's back. It landed about three feet in front of the man's feet.

"Why are you doing this?" Colbert asked. "I'm no Yankee. I just ferry my customers across the river."

"Yeah, well, we're not going to ferry no customers," said the man who had spoken first. "We're only going to ferry Confederate soldiers. This here is a military installation from now on."

While the man was talking, the one in front of Dhu bent to pick up the gun Dhu had tossed. The attention of the other three was all concentrated on Colbert. Dhu slipped his right hand into his saddlebag and found the extra revolver. He pulled it out of the bag and cocked it at the same time. Swinging it up over the saddle, he fired just as the man nearest him was straightening up. The man fell backwards with an astonished expression on his face and a gaping hole in the center of his chest. At the sound of the shot, the other three turned to face Dhu, and Colbert jumped into the river.

Dhu's second shot smashed the right shoulder of the man who seemed to be in charge. Then he threw himself to his right and backwards, sliding down the muddy bank of the river, going into the water up to his waist. With his left hand he clutched the grass on the edge of the bank to keep himself from going all the way in. Only his head and shoulders were visible to the three remaining gunmen. Two of them fired as they ran toward him, but their shots went wild. Dhu fired again and hit one man low in the abdomen. The man doubled up and rolled over as if turning a somersault. The other, realizing he was alone, turned to flee. Dhu put a bullet in his back. Then he looked over at the one with the smashed shoulder. He was sitting on the ground clutching his wound. Blood ran freely through his fingers and down his arm and chest. Dhu didn't want to shoot the man again. He was helpless there. But what would he do with him? If he let the man go, there would likely be reprisals against Colbert. He swung his revolver around and aimed it at the man. The man's bloody left hand groped for the revolver lying on the ground before him. He growled like a wounded animal. That made it easier for Dhu, and he squeezed the trigger. The shot hit the man in the forehead, snapping his head back, then forward again. The man's chin dropped to his chest. His body sagged for an instant, then fell over to one side.

Dhu dragged himself back up onto the bank and looked at the four gunmen. They were all dead. He stuck the revolver in his belt and trotted over to the ferry. Looking upriver, he saw Colbert's head sticking out of the water.

"Come on," he said. "It's over."

Colbert splashed back toward the ferry

and reached a hand up for Dhu to grasp. Dhu pulled him up onto the ferry.

"Thanks, young fellow," said Colbert. "If you hadn't been here I'd probably be dead by now. You can forget about them four saddles. I'll ferry you across for nothing anytime you want to go. You and whoever or whatever you got with you."

"The saddles are yours," said Dhu. "If we take a look around, I'll bet we find four more — on the horses that these four rode. You can have them, too, and the horses, if you want them. There is something you could do for me, though."

"Name it," said Colbert.

Dhu told Colbert a little about his plan to ambush Captain Early's patrol. He told him how they wanted to steer Early's command to a ford downriver.

"I hate to disable your ferry," he said, "but it's the only thing we could come up with. When it's all over with, we'll pay you for the damages. I'll even help you fix it back up."

"Hell," said Colbert. "It ain't going to be that tough. I can discombobulate this thing real easy, and in such a way that I can put it back together even easier. You just let me know when that bunch is coming through, and I'll do her."

"Good," said Dhu. "Let's go round up those horses, and I'll get rid of these four bodies for you. Then I'll be on my way."

12

Mary Beth sat on one of the horses Dhu and Ben had left. She was at the edge of the woods, watching the road that led across the prairie to her house. Her father and brother had gone to the ford, and her father had said she should keep an eye out in case those ruffians decided to come back.

Now she saw them coming, six of them off in the distance. There was no other place for them to be going, not on that road heading in her direction. She knew it was them coming back to try again. There was no way for her to get to her father in time. She raced the horse back to the house and ran inside.

"They're coming, Mama," she said. "Six of them."

"All right," Maude said. "Let's go."

Maude picked up a rifle and a six-gun, and so did Mary Beth. They went outside and mounted up double on the horse and rode back out to where Mary Beth had been. They took the horse into the woods and tied it. Mary Beth got behind a tree, and Maude crossed the lane and got behind another. They waited. The riders came closer. Still they waited. "Until you can see the whites of their eyes," Maude had said. At last Maude squeezed off a round, and it knocked the hat off a rider's head. The riders reined up quickly and turned their mounts. They rode back down the road a little way. Mary Beth fired a shot just as they were turning, and her bullet tore the jacket at a man's shoulder. He gave a yelp and spurred his horse. When the riders thought they were beyond shooting range, they stopped and turned their mounts again. They sat there, undecided, looking toward the woods. In the stillness, their voices carried on down to Mary Beth and Maude.

"They must still have them reinforcements in there," said one.

"How many, you reckon?"

"I don't know, but they like to have killed us all the last time."

"We need more men."

"They ain't no more to get. They're either dead or off in the army."

"They're all through them trees down there."

"It's going to take a troop of cavalry to get to them."

"What do you say?"

"Let's get the hell out of here."

The riders turned once more and rode away. Maude stepped out into the lane and watched as they slowly vanished.

"That'll teach them," she said. "If they try it again, they'll get worse."

Ben saw some riders coming toward him on the road. They were still a good distance off. He couldn't tell anything about them except that it was a fair-size group of men, maybe eight or ten, and they were riding at a leisurely pace. They might be soldiers, he thought.

There was no cover of any kind, just the rolling prairie. He couldn't fight them alone. He knew that. He jerked the reins, turned his horse to his right, and beat a trail west through the dry grass. He wondered if the horsemen had seen him. He had no way of knowing, but if he had seen them, he had to assume that they might just as easily have spotted him. He rode hard, getting as far off the road as possible before the riders came close. The only change he could see in the terrain as he rode west was that he was no longer following a road. He kept looking off to his left to see where the riders were, and he noted with pleasure that the distance between them was growing. They were not increasing their pace. Either they had not seen him or they didn't care. He rode a little farther, then stopped to take a look. He was surprised to find that the land was not as flat as he had thought. He had lost sight of the riders and the road. He turned his horse around and moved back to the top of what appeared to be just a slight rise. Then he saw them. He could tell that it was a squad of cavalry. They seemed unaware of his presence. He turned south again, feeling good that he had just avoided a confrontation with the enemy.

When he headed back to the road, he saw the outlines of a small town ahead. He thought about circling around it, but his canteen was low on water, and his horse needed a drink. There would be water in a town. The prairie had been dry and dusty, and he had found no streams for a good many miles. He decided to take a chance on the town. He got back on the road and went straight ahead.

It was a sleepy little town. A woman was going into a general store, and four old men were sitting in a row in front of the bank. They were all chewing tobacco and spitting on the street. Two of them were whittling on sticks. Ben didn't see any trees anywhere, and he wondered where they'd gotten the sticks. Two small boys ran along the street rolling a hoop. The saloon appeared to be open for business.

Ben rode straight to the first water trough he saw and let the horse drink. He took his canteen off the saddle and worked the pump handle to get fresh water for himself. When he had filled his canteen and replaced it, he dipped his hands in the water and bathed his face. He had just straightened up and was daubing the water from his eyes with his sleeve when he heard a voice very near.

"Stranger in town, eh?" it said.

He lowered his arm and blinked his eyes. "Just passing through," he said. "Needed some water for my horse."

"Where you headed, stranger?"

It was a young man, not much older than Ben. He had the look of a cowboy, Ben thought. He wore a gun belt with a six-shooter hanging at his left hip, butt forward. A cross-draw artist, Ben thought. A gunfighter.

"South," Ben said.

"Where'bouts south?"

"Mister," said Ben, afraid his voice was noticeably quavering, "I was raised to believe that this is a free country. Like I said,

I'm just riding through."

He turned to mount his horse, but the other man stepped up and grabbed him by the shoulder, pulling him back around.

"These are bad times, stranger," said the man. "War's going on. I asked you where you're going."

"I don't want no trouble here," said Ben. "Now just back off and let me alone."

"You got the sound of a Yankee to me." The man took another step toward Ben.

Ben didn't wait to see what the man might have in mind. He swung a hard surprise left, catching the man on the side of the head and sending him staggering to one side. Before the man had time to recover, Ben had pulled the revolver out of his belt.

The man straightened up and saw the gun barrel pointed at him. He stood still. "Put it back," he said, "and let's see who's the fastest."

"I ain't no gunfighter, mister," said Ben. "If you want to have it out with me, drop that gun belt to the ground. I'll put this here aside, and we'll slug it out right here in the street."

A small crowd had gathered by that time on the sidewalk to watch the proceedings, and the gunman was well aware of their presence. He had been challenged. His reputation was at stake. "All right," he said. "We'll do it your way." He unfastened the gun belt and tossed it up on the boardwalk.

Ben went over to the boardwalk and set his revolver down. Then he stepped back out into the street and stood there waiting, hands hanging loose at his sides, eyes fastened on his opponent.

The Texan grinned and raised his fists and began circling Ben. As he circled, he moved in closer.

Ben stood waiting, turning as his opponent circled. Finally the Texan swung a vicious but wild right, which Ben easily ducked. Still bent over, Ben drove a fist hard into the gunfighter's midsection, forcing all the air out of the man's lungs. The Texan doubled over, gasping for breath. He tried desperately to stay on his feet, but his knees buckled and he sank to the ground. Ben could easily have moved in for the kill, could have pounded the cocky Texan to a pulp before he ever regained his breath. Instead, he turned away and retrieved his revolver, then walked over to his horse and gathered up the reins. He put a foot in the stirrup and swung up into the saddle, then turned the horse and began to ride on through town.

The small crowd was obviously disappointed. The fight they had anticipated had ended with one punch. The stranger was riding out of town. It was all over — at least they thought it was all over.

The Texan began to catch his breath, and he stood up. He saw Ben riding away from him. He turned and looked at the crowd and saw the scorn in their faces. Furious, he ran to the boardwalk and jerked his revolver from its holster. He turned, aimed the revolver, and pulled the trigger.

"Hey," someone in the crowd shouted.

Ben felt the slug tear a piece out of his ear at the same time he heard the shot. The whole side of his head burned with the pain, but his thoughts were remarkably clear. He spurred his horse and raced around to the far side of a small wooden building, then quickly dismounted and pulled the rifle from its scabbard.

He ran to the corner of the building and peered around. The Texan saw him and fired another shot, but Ben ducked back behind the building, and the bullet kicked splinters off the wood. Ben pulled back the hammer on his rifle. He took a deep breath, then stepped out from behind his cover, the rifle to his shoulder. He took aim quickly. The enraged Texan fired again, but his shot went wild, and Ben pulled the trigger.

The heavy rifle ball slammed into the man's chest, causing him to jerk convulsively from the waist up. He looked down at the hole in his chest with disbelief. Blood gushed freely from the ghastly wound. He staggered backward two, three steps, and then stopped and swayed. At last he fell forward straight as a board, landing hard on his face and bouncing once before he lay there still and dead.

Ben's single-shot rifle was empty. He shifted it to his left hand and pulled the revolver out of his belt with his right. He looked toward the crowd anxiously, wondering if anyone was about to take up the fight on his fallen comrade's behalf. He wondered if he would have to fight the whole town. He thought about Dhu and their mission, and then he thought about Mary Beth and her beauty, and he wondered what the future might have been like for him if he'd had the good sense to ride around this jerkwater Texas town.

A big man stepped out from the crowd on the sidewalk and took a few strides into the street, moving slowly in Ben's direction. He held his hands out to his sides.

"Stranger," he called out to Ben.

Ben pointed his revolver in the man's direction. He stood poised, ready for more action.

"Stranger, it's all right," said the man. "We're all witnesses. It was self-defense. Halleck there, he's been asking for that for a long time now. You can ride on out in comfort. Ain't no one here going to give you no trouble."

Ben wasn't sure he should believe the man. He looked the crowd over. They all appeared to be pretty much relaxed. No one was holding a gun or even going for one. He shot a look back over his shoulder to locate his horse; then he backed up to it. He looked again at the crowd of Texans, tucked the revolver into his belt, and mounted up. He rode out of town without looking back again.

13

When Ben finally spotted Old Harm it startled him. Perhaps he had been thinking he would never really see the man and his patrol. Maybe he felt that he was simply riding an endless trail south with no real goal, no purpose in mind.

The Texas landscape had changed. The rolling ground had turned to rolling hills dotted with trees. He had actually crossed a small stream with running water. Then he topped a rise and there they were, Early and eight of his soldiers. Seven of the troopers were mounted. The eighth was driving a team of four horses hitched to a wagon. Four horses meant a heavy load. They had the gold. The driver's horse was tied to the back of the wagon.

In his astonishment, Ben just sat there in the middle of the road for a while taking in the scene before him. Then he came to his senses and moved into the cover of some large pecan trees. He backed away from the road a safe distance and waited while the gold escort came closer and finally passed him by. Still he waited to allow them to get a distance ahead of him. Then he moved out on the road and followed slowly.

When the sun set, the rebels made camp. Ben had dropped back so far that he couldn't actually see them up ahead, but he saw their fires. He didn't want to make his presence known to them, so he settled down for the night with no fire, ate cold food, and slept rolled in his blanket.

In the morning he risked a fire and made himself some coffee, but he didn't bother to cook any breakfast, just eating cold biscuits instead. He put out the fire and saddled and packed his horse, then mounted up and rode ahead. When he spotted the patrol moving out, he slowed down again. He had just wanted to make sure they were still there.

For the rest of that day he followed them, letting them stay out of his sight most of the time but riding up closer every now and then to check on their continued presence on the road ahead of him.

The following morning he decided they had nowhere left to go except north to Colbert's ferry and the Texas Road beyond. He cut east across the prairie to circle wide around the patrol. He would ride ahead of them to meet Dhu back at the McClellans' place and set up the ambush. It should be no problem. There were nine rebels, and there would be nine attackers, including Herd and Sam Ed McClellan.

Ben rode fast. He not only wanted to get back well ahead of Old Harm, he was also anxious to see Mary Beth again.

When Dhu arrived at Middle Striker's house, everyone was there except Ketch Barnett.

"He's gone to Tahlequah," said Middle Striker. "He should be back here in the morning."

Dhu's ride north had been uneventful. He had hidden from a couple of small parties of riders along the road. They might not have been Confederates, but he had thought it best to avoid them just in case. He had circled around one large party, which he had felt pretty sure was a military unit of some kind. He was glad to have the trip over and done with and glad that on the return trip he would have some company. There would be six going back. He was also pleased to fill his belly with the good Cherokee cooking of Middle Striker's wife.

He explained the plan to Middle Striker

and the others, told them how Ben had gone farther south to locate the gold escort, how they would meet back at the river at the home of the McClellans, new allies they had met, how Old Harm's troop would be directed away from the ferry with Colbert's cooperation, and how McClellan was preparing an ambush site at the ford on his own property.

"We should start south in the morning," he said, "when Ketch gets back."

"We're all ready to go," Middle Striker told him.

"Mama," Mary Beth asked, "do you like Ben?"

"What kind of a question is that?" Maude said. "Of course I like him, both him and Dhu. They're good boys, polite and hardworking. And they probably saved our lives that first night they showed up."

"Oh, I know all that, Mama, but I mean do you really like Ben?"

Maude looked up from her work. She was shelling peas from the garden. She furrowed her brow and studied her daughter's face for a moment. "Yes, Mary Beth, I like him," she said.

"*Really* like him?"

"I said I like him, child. What more do

you want me to say?"

"I'm not a child anymore," said Mary Beth.

Maude went back to her work. "No, I guess you're not."

Mary Beth blushed slightly and ducked her head, looking at her hands in her lap rather than at her mother. "I think he likes me," she said.

"I should think so," Maude said. "You're a nice girl — a nice young woman. That's the way we've raised you. Anybody would like you."

"I mean more than that, Mama," Mary Beth said. "I mean — Excuse me, Mama." She got up, jerked the front door open, and went outside, shutting the door behind her.

Maude looked up at the door, staring after her daughter. She sat like that for a long moment, then heaved a slow and heavy sigh.

"That's plenty, Sam Ed," said McClellan. "Let's get this brush picked up."

Herd and Sam Ed had cleared out narrow, nearly imperceptible paths through the woods on both sides of the river leading to places of concealment for nine men, four on the Texas side of the river and five on the Indian Territory side. As they cut brush each day, they loaded it in the wagon and hauled it away. There would be no evidence of the work that had gone on in the woods. The only indication of any recent activity in the area would be the obviously recent wagon tracks to the ford, and their explanation would be that people were fording the river because Colbert's ferry was out of commission. When Dhu and the others were in their hiding places, the rebel gold escort should ride right down to the river and start to cross without suspecting anything amiss.

McClellan was proud of his work and of the planning that had gone into it. He and Sam Ed loaded the freshly cut brush into the wagon and headed for home, taking care to drive over the same tracks they had been wearing through the grass for the last few days.

Gordon Early sat straight in the saddle, his chin held high, his black stallion prancing at the head of the little Confederate column. His sergeant rode to his left and just a little behind. Then came the wagon, driven by a private, his horse tied to the rear of the wagon. Two troopers rode on either side of the wagon, and two more brought up the rear. Early's sword clanked at his side as he rode, and the long white plume waving above his wide-brimmed hat gave him the look of a swash-buckling buccaneer.

"Sergeant," Early said, "that looks like a small town up ahead."

"Yes, sir, I remember it from the trip down."

"Send a man ahead to check it out."

"Yes, sir." The sergeant called out to one of the men. "Turner!"

A private spurred his horse forward. "Yes, Sergeant," he said.

"Ride into that town and look the place over. Then come back and tell us what you found."

"Yes, Sergeant."

Private Turner raced ahead while the rest of the escort maintained its leisurely pace. Soon the private returned. He reined in just ahead of Early and the sergeant and saluted.

Early snapped back a neat salute. "Report to the sergeant," he said.

"Yes, sir." The private turned his horse and fell in beside the sergeant. "Just a quiet little town, Sergeant," he said. "Not much going on. There's a bank and a general store. A saloon. A couple more businesses. Oh, yeah, a livery stable. I saw a few old men sitting around not doing much and a couple of women looked like they were shopping. There were a few men inside the saloon. That's about it."

"No military presence?" Early said without turning his head.

"No, sir."

"Return to your post, Private," said the sergeant.

"It's getting late, Sergeant," Early said. "We'll rest tonight in that town. We may even allow ourselves a little refreshment in that saloon."

The small-town Texans welcomed the smartlooking Confederate soldiers with cheers, and the owner of the saloon greeted them with a broad toothy smile.

"Do you serve food in here, sir?" Early asked.

"Yes, indeed, Captain," the proprietor said. "Lon Draper here, at your service. I have a kitchen in the back."

"Captain Gordon Early, Confederate States Army," said Early. "Put on nine of your best steaks and break out a bottle of your best Bourbon County whiskey."

"Right away, Captain Early."

Early turned to his sergeant.

"Sergeant," he said, "you and I can have a couple of drinks, but we must remain sober. We'll let the troops have a real toot, though."

"Yes, sir," said the sergeant.

The soldiers had the best meal they had eaten in a long while, and then proceeded to get drunk. A couple of them passed out early, and the others got a bit rowdy, but with Early and the sergeant watching over them, things never got out of control. Late in the evening, Early called a halt to the festivities.

"Sergeant," he said, "take the men down to the end of the street and make camp. We'll give them two extra hours of sleep in the morning, and then we'll be off."

"Yes, sir," said the sergeant, and he gathered up his drunken charges and left the saloon. Lon Draper presented Early with a bill.

"I'd like all my men to have breakfast here in the morning, Mr. Draper," said Early. "Can you provide that meal?"

"If ham and eggs and taters will satisfy you, yes," said Draper.

"And coffee," said Early. "Lots of coffee."

"Of course."

"Very well," said Early. "I'll see you then,

and we'll settle the entire bill all at once."

"I, uh, well, yeah," said Draper. "I guess that'll be all right."

Early was already mounted on his prancing black stallion, and the sergeant was shouting orders. The troopers were a little sluggish, but they were getting the work done, breaking camp and packing to move out. Early walked his stallion over to the wagon and dismounted. He lifted a corner of the canvas cover and saw the early morning sun glint off the corner of a bar of gold. He put his hand on the bar and felt it, cold and hard and smooth, and he considered in his mind the vast fortune that had been placed in his charge. It was enough, he thought, to corrupt a saint, and Gordon Early, Old Harm, was no saint. He pulled the canvas back down and rode away a few yards, then turned to survey his troops. When they were packed, Early led them back to Draper's establishment, and they all went inside. The wagon was parked just outside a large front window, so Early could see it at all times. The troopers sat down. Early remained standing, his sergeant at his side. Draper walked up to meet him.

"Good morning, Mr. Draper," said

Early. "Bring on the breakfast."

"I hope," said Draper, "that you're prepared to pay me for all this in hard, cold cash."

"A chit signed by an officer in the Army of the Confederate States of America is good enough for anyone in the South, sir," said Early.

"Captain Early, sir, I been paid in them chits before, and I ain't never been able to get my money out of them. If you ain't prepared to pay your bill in hard cash, you can just ride on out of here hungry, by God, you and your whole damn crew."

Early paced away from Draper. He stood for a moment at the window, looking out at the wagon, thinking of the gold just there underneath the canvas, thinking of the war and of the Confederacy and fantasizing about a life of wealth and ease and luxury. Then he turned back fast, giving Draper a hard, steady stare.

"Get the breakfast started, Mr. Draper," he said. "You'll be paid. Come along with me. I want to show you something."

Draper told the cook to prepare the meal, and he followed Early outside. Early led him around to the far side of the canvas-covered wagon bed.

"Mr. Draper," he said, "how do you like the feel of gold?"

"I ain't felt much of it," said Draper, "but I think I'd like it fine."

"Did you ever wonder why nine cavalrymen were escorting a wagon through your little town, Mr. Draper? Did you notice how low this wagon is riding? Did you wonder why such a small wagon was being pulled by four horses?"

Draper's eyes opened wide and he stepped in closer to Early. "Gold?" he whispered.

"Gold, Mr. Draper. Is there any problem with my bill?"

"Hell no, Captain. No problem at all."

"Then let's get back to your establishment. I, too, need to eat."

They went back to Draper's establishment, and Early got his meal. He was the last one to finish eating, and when he had drunk the last of his coffee, he motioned to the sergeant.

"Yes, sir?"

"Take the men over to the general store and get them all new civilian clothes," said Early. "I'll take care of the bill here and then join you. I need a new outfit, too."

The sergeant looked puzzled, but he said, "Yes, sir."

Then he gathered the men and left the saloon, and Early walked toward Draper, who was waiting greedily.

"Mr. Draper," said Early, "do you have a private room where we can do business?"

"Right this way," said Draper. He led Early to a door at the back of the saloon and opened it. "My office," he said.

"After you," said Early.

Draper walked in, and Early followed him and shut the door. The saloon keeper moved around behind his desk. Early turned to face him, revolver in hand and pointed at him.

Draper's mouth dropped open. His eyes were big. "What — what is this?" he said.

Early pulled the trigger, and a lead ball tore through Draper's chest. Draper staggered back against the wall and stood for an instant. Then he fell forward across his desk. Slowly he slipped off and crumpled in a heap behind the desk. There was a trail of blood on the desktop and a blotch on the wall behind him. Early holstered the revolver and left the office.

14

As Ben rode well ahead of Old Harm and his men on the road to the Red River, the reality of the impending situation finally settled in his mind. Before, it had all seemed remote and unreal, but as he hurried back to Herd McClellan's farm to meet Dhu, Ben knew that it was actually going to happen. They were going to lie in wait to kill those men.

He tried to imagine how it would happen. Old Harm and his men would ride into the middle of the Red River. Dhu, the five Indians, Ben, McClellan, and Sam Ed would open fire. The nine Confederate soldiers would be dead almost before they knew what had happened. It would be a slaughter. It didn't seem like war. Not really. War was what it had been like at Elkhorn Tavern, where Ben had been part of a team of men operating a cannon, where there were officers who made plans and other officers who shouted orders, where there was an army on one side of the field and an army on the other side of the field and they were shooting at each other. Ben argued with himself. Did he want to send a message to Old Harm before the rebels reached the woods there by the river, informing him that there were Union soldiers waiting? Did he want to challenge Early to meet them in open combat on the prairie? He didn't know what he wanted. He wished the war had never started.

But if the war had not started, he would never have come to Texas and met Mary Beth. If he could survive this ambush, maybe something good would come out of the war after all. He wondered how Mary Beth was doing. He knew there was a strong possibility that the McClellans' hostile rebel neighbors would stage another attack. He hoped she was safe, and he wondered if she was thinking about him, worrying about his safety, as he was about hers.

Dhu and the other four Pins were packed and ready to go. They had checked their weapons, parceled out the ammunition, saddled the horses, and strapped on their blanket rolls. They were only waiting for the return of Ketch Barnett.

"He should have been back by now," said Middle Striker.

"If he doesn't show up pretty soon," said Dhu, "we'd better go without him. There's still five of us. Ben makes six, and the two McClellans makes eight. Colbert said there were only nine rebels, and we'll be catching them totally by surprise. We can go without Barnett if we have to."

He was pacing the floor nervously and feeling agitated. He felt some resentment building up inside him toward Ketch. He then realized that he had become obsessed with the idea of attacking Old Harm and getting the gold. He was looking forward to the clash at the river. It wasn't the war that had given rise to his obsession. It wasn't the Union cause. It was not even bitterness over what the southern states had done to the Cherokee Nation. It was personal: Dhu and Old Harm.

He was about ready to suggest that they forget about Ketch Barnett and get started when Hair spoke up.

"Somebody's coming," he said.

They all waited without saying anything more, and in a few minutes Barnett rode into the yard.

"I'm sorry, Dhu," he said. "The five of us can't go with you."

"Why not?" Dhu said.

"I just got word from Captain Phillips," said Barnett. "We're needed up north of here. There's a bunch of refugees, Cherokees and Creeks mostly, whole families, women and kids and old folks. Some of them are sick. They're trying to get up to Kansas to get out of this war, and they need us to be their armed escort, because there's a troop of Confederate Cherokees riding to intercept them."

"Why do the Confederates want to stop these people?" said Middle Striker.

"Who knows?" Barnett said. "All I know is that Captain Phillips says that we need to get there right away to escort those people to safety."

Middle Striker turned to face Dhu. "Old Harm is still coming," he said, "and he's got all that gold for the South."

"That's not your worry now," said Dhu. "We'll just have to find a way to manage without you."

"Good luck to you, Dhu," said Barnett.

All five of the Pins had mounted their horses and were ready to ride: Ketch Barnett, Middle Striker, Bird-in-Close, and Bear-at-Home. Dhu looked at them; they were looking at the ground. He knew they hated to let him down, but the call from their captain had to take precedence, and the helpless refugees needed their protection. Dhu understood.

"And good luck to you, too," he said.

The Pins turned their horses and rode away, leaving Dhu alone in front of the house deep in the woods.

Riding the Texas Road, alone once again, Dhu still wanted to get Old Harm. He had never really cared that much about stopping the delivery of gold to the Confederacy. He had cared about preventing Old Harm from accomplishing his mission. Now Old Harm was down there in Texas with all that gold, and Dhu and Ben would not have the help of the Cherokee Pins. There were only four of them now to stop Old Harm — Dhu, Ben, McClellan, and Sam Ed — and Sam Ed was just a boy, a boy who could shoot and had already killed a man, true enough, but still just a boy. Four against nine. They could still manage it, he reasoned, if they set up the ambush just right and if they lured Old Harm into the trap exactly the way McClellan had planned.

And what about the gold? Dhu didn't care. He would let Ben or McClellan have it. They could split it between them or take it to the United States government if they were so inclined. Or they could let it sink into the Red River for all Dhu cared. The more he thought about it, the more anxious he became to get to the McClellan place, but he knew better than to push the horse too hard.

He wondered how Ben had fared on his own down in Texas, and he realized, to his own surprise, that he was worried about the Iowan. If he had it to do over again, he thought, he wouldn't let Ben go down there by himself. Dhu might just as well have stayed in Texas and accompanied Ben south to scout for Old Harm. But of course he hadn't known what would happen with the Pins. It was always easy to say what one would have done if one had only known.

"Papa," said Mary Beth, "when do you think Ben will get back?"

"I don't know," McClellan said. "It all depends on how far south he had to ride to find them rebels."

"He will be back, won't he? You don't think anything could have happened to him?"

"Anything could happen to anybody these days. There's a war going on," McClellan said. "But Ben's a pretty shrewd lad. He can look out for himself."

"Yeah," said Mary Beth. "I think I'll walk out the path and keep Sam Ed company for a while."

Mary Beth left the house and ambled toward the spot where the trees bordered the prairie, the spot where they kept watch for hostile neighbors. Under the pretense of helping Sam Ed watch out for their enemies, she could wait for the return of Ben.

When Mary Beth had closed the door behind herself, Herd McClellan looked at his wife, a puzzled expression on his face. "Maude," he said, "did you notice anything funny in the way Mary Beth was talking?"

"What do you mean, Herd?"

"Well, she was asking about Ben, but she never said nothing about Dhu. Both of them boys is out there in some danger, I'd say, but she didn't say nothing about Dhu. Don't she like him? It ain't because he's Indian, is it? I know she ain't never been around Indians, but that Dhu is a nice young fellow, and he is half white."

"Herd," said Maude, "sometimes you don't show no more brains than a prairie chicken."

"What do you mean by that, woman?"

"Mary Beth is in love, Herd."

"With Ben?"

"With Ben."

"But she's just a child." McClellan's look

combined sadness with something akin to horror.

"She's a young woman, Herd. It's natural."

McClellan leaned back heavily in his chair and stared at the wall across the room, his jaw slack. "Well," he said, "I'll be damned."

"Watch your language in my house, Herd."

As Gordon Early led his men out of town in their new outfits, townspeople lined the sidewalks to stare at them. They stood and watched the nine men ride out of town, and then they looked at one another.

"I thought they was soldiers," said one.

"Well," said another, "I reckon they got their reasons. Maybe they're going under cover or something."

"I heard two gunshots."

A gray-haired man with a badge pinned on his vest stepped forward. "I asked them about that just as they was a leaving," he said. "The captain told me he was checking his revolver out behind the saloon. Said he'd dropped it, and he wanted to make sure it was shooting right."

The cook sneaked a look out the front

door of Lon Draper's saloon and saw the crowd gathered on the sidewalk. "Are they gone?" he asked one of the onlookers.

"Them soldiers?" said one of the men. "Yeah, they're gone. All dressed up like civilians now, though."

"They killed Lon," said the cook. "I been hiding back there so they wouldn't kill me, too."

"Where is he?" said the man with the badge. The whole crowd turned to follow the cook back into the saloon, but before they had made any progress, a woman screamed somewhere down the street. They turned again to find the source of this new horror, and they saw her in front of the general store. They started moving toward her.

"What is it?" someone shouted.

"Oliver's dead," said the woman. "Right in there. He's dead."

A quick investigation revealed that the soldiers had killed Lon Draper and the owner of the general store, apparently to avoid paying their bills at those two establishments.

Soon all of the townspeople were in the street, all talking at once. Finally the man with the badge stepped up on the sidewalk, pulled out his revolver, and fired two shots into the air. The crowd quieted down and faced him. He stuck the gun back into its old worn holster.

"Now, let's all calm down," he said. "Where's Albert?"

A man in the crowd waved his arm. "Right here, Harv."

"Albert, take care of them two bodies. We can't just leave them lay there."

"All right." Albert shoved his way out of the crowd to go about his business.

"I've got to go after those men," Harv said, "and I ain't got much chance of taking them all by myself. Now, I know the war took might near all our young men, but I need a posse. Anyone able and willing to go with me, get your horse and gun and meet me at my office in a half an hour. The rest of you go on about your business."

The lawman turned and walked to his office. He replaced the two bullets he had fired into the air, took a rifle out of a case on the wall, loaded it, and filled his pockets with extra ammunition. Then he walked to the livery stable and saddled a horse. In half an hour he was back at his office, mounted and ready to go. Harvey Eubanks was a twenty-year veteran of law enforcement in Texas, and he had seen plenty of action in his day. But sitting in the saddle there in front of his office, he felt his age. He dreaded the long, hard ride after the nine fugitives, and even more he dreaded the fight he knew would follow.

He was beginning to think he would have to ride after the outlaws alone when two riders came toward him on the street. One was the cook from Draper's saloon, the other a bank teller.

"Hello, Mel," Eubanks said. "Bob. Thanks for coming."

"There's two more coming," said Bob, the teller. "Lynn Jones and Bill Day."

Eubanks heaved a sigh. These were not fighting men. All of them were as old as he was, except Mel, who was in his forties. He wondered if any of them could even shoot straight.

"That's good," he said.

Just then Day and Jones appeared at the other end of the street. When Eubanks had all four men together, he nudged his horse forward and moved out in front of them, then turned to face them.

"I appreciate you men showing up," he said, "but I want to emphasize that we're riding out after nine hard young men — soldiers, it seems, though I don't know why soldiers would murder Lou and Oliver. They're well armed, and they're killers. I won't hold it against any of you if you change your minds."

He paused for a response but there was none.

"All right," he said. "Let's go."

The little posse began to ride. They had not gone half a mile out of town when they heard horses coming up fast behind them.

Lynn Jones turned to see what it was. "It's Little Joe and Acey," he said.

"Wait up." Eubanks furrowed his brow in an expression of pain. Here were two young men coming to join in the chase, two cowboys from a nearby ranch. He had been concerned that his posse was too old. But these two were wild and undisciplined. Oh, well, he thought, they're two more bodies. A man can't always have everything his way.

15

Ben had imagined a tender reunion with Mary Beth. When he arrived at the McClellans' farm, however, Dhu was already there, and everyone greeted him at once.

"Did you find them?" McClellan asked.

"Yeah," Ben said. "They're coming this way, just like we figured."

"How far back?" said Dhu.

"I'd say they're at least a day and a half behind me," said Ben. "Maybe two days. They're moving pretty slow with that wagon."

"Then we've got time to let Ben eat," Maude said. "You men can talk business later. Come on in the house, Ben. I'll get you something to eat."

"Thanks," said Ben. He shot a glance in Mary Beth's direction.

She smiled and looked down at the ground. "I'll help you, Mama," she said.

On the way into the house, Ben glanced at Dhu. "Where's the Pins?" he said.

"They're not coming," said Dhu. "It's just us."

Ben had reached the table by then, but he did not sit down. For a moment he thought that his original impression of Indians must have been accurate. They couldn't be depended on, couldn't be trusted. "What'd they back out for?" he said.

"They had no choice," Dhu said. "They got orders to escort a bunch of civilians up to Kansas."

Ben dropped into his chair. "Well, that's it, then," he said. "We was counting on them."

Thoughts raced through his mind and entangled themselves with one another. He could go back and try to find his outfit, but back where? He had no idea where they might be. He could just go home, forget about Old Harm and the rebel soldiers and their foreign gold. Forget about fighting. Forget the whole damn war. He could look forward to making his own life. The future lay ahead of him, inviting and exciting. Maude put a cup of coffee in front of him.

"Thank you," he said absentmindedly. He stared ahead, his expression blank. He had been a soldier, and he had been a prisoner. If he failed to return to the army, he would be a deserter. But the army probably thought he was dead or in a rebel prison camp. He was deep in enemy territory, and he had no idea what he should do. He wanted to talk to Mary Beth, but she was helping her mother prepare a meal for him, and everyone else was huddled near them. He was irritated with them all of a sudden. Why didn't they go away and leave him alone with Mary Beth? She put a plate of food in front of him.

"Thank you," he said again. He ate, but he hardly knew what he was eating. His mind was somewhere else. Mary Beth refilled his cup.

"Well," said Ben, "like I told you, Old Harm is coming this way with all that gold. I stayed with him long enough to see that there wasn't no other way for him to go, unless he decided to cut across the prairie. But if the Pins ain't coming down to help us, I guess it don't matter none. I guess we ain't got no more mission." He looked around the room. Everyone was silent.

Dhu helped himself to a cup of coffee and sat down at the table directly across from Ben. "Who does that gold belong to, Ben?" he said.

"It's foreign gold. From some foreign country. It's being sent to the Confederate government."

"If it never gets to the Confederacy,"

said Dhu, "we've accomplished our mission. Right? It doesn't have to get to the United States, does it? It never belonged to the U.S. anyway."

"Well, I — I don't know. I guess you're right. But what difference does that make? We're through."

"We don't need the Pins," Dhu said.

"What do you mean?" Ben was incredulous. "What do you mean we don't need them? There's nine of them rebels, and there's just only four of us."

Dhu looked at McClellan. "What do you think?" he said.

"I don't know," said the old man. "I ain't got the personal feelings against this Early that you boys has got, and the odds ain't as good as we thought they'd be. I'm thinking on it."

Dhu stared across the table at Ben. Among the Cherokees, staring was considered rude, even threatening, but Dhu knew that whites had different ways, so he stared. Sam Ed stood back against the wall looking as if he'd like to join the conversation, but he kept quiet.

"I need to think on it, damn it," said Ben. "I need to think on it, too."

He gave Mary Beth a pitiful look, and she took the hint.

"Let's go for a walk, Ben," she said. Then she looked at her mother. "All right?"

"Go on," said Maude.

Ben and Mary Beth went outside, and Dhu turned his attention to Herd McClellan.

"Herd," he said, "do I recall hearing you say you wanted to raise horses?"

"I wouldn't be surprised," said McClellan. "I might have said it. It's the truth. I love horses, and raising horses would be a good business. A whole lot better'n this scratching in the dirt."

"That gold would sure give you a good start," Dhu said.

"Yeah. It sure would."

"The way I see it, taking that shipment wouldn't be like stealing. That gold doesn't belong to anyone. The Confederacy has no right to exist. If it did, we wouldn't be at war. So the gold can't belong to them. It might just as well be ours."

"What you say makes a lot of sense," McClellan said. "But there's nine of them fellows."

"Yeah, and just two of us if you back out."

"Three," said McClellan. "I'll go along."

"Three? Now, Herd, I'm not trying to force you to throw in with us on this."

"What's the matter?" McClellan said. "You don't think there's enough gold to go around? You don't think it'll split three ways?"

Dhu had accomplished his purpose with McClellan. He stood and walked toward the front door. "I don't give a damn about the gold," he said. Then, turning back to face McClellan, he added, "I want to stop Old Harm. That's all I care about."

"What about the war?" McClellan asked.

"It's your war," Dhu said. "Not mine."

"Well, if we get that gold," said McClellan, "we stop Old Harm. That'll satisfy you. We help the Union by keeping the gold from the rebels. That should satisfy any nationalistic cravings me and Ben might have. And we get the gold. That thought satisfies me total."

"It's still nine against three," Dhu said.

"Four," said Sam Ed, who had been quiet through all the long debate.

Dhu looked at McClellan. The old man had a stern expression set on his face as he studied his son. Then he looked back at Dhu and nodded.

"Four," he said.

"That's two rebels apiece and one left

over," said Dhu. "If we can catch them in the trap you laid, we can handle them."

McClellan turned to his son and put a hand on his shoulder. "Boy," he said, "this ain't exactly what we thought it would be when we started out. I ain't going to hold you to it if you don't want to go through with it."

"Let's do it, Papa," said Sam Ed.

Outside Ben and Mary Beth had walked to the end of the lane. They stood together in silence for a moment, looking out across the prairie. Ben thought it looked vast and lonesome. He wanted to put an arm around Mary Beth, but he was afraid to.

"What are you thinking, Ben?" Mary Beth said.

Her voice surprised him, and he almost jumped.

"I don't know exactly," he said. "I guess I'm wondering what to do. I don't know where my outfit's at. I should try to find them, I guess. I just don't know."

"If you tried to find them," said Mary Beth, "where would you start looking? How would you go about it?"

"I don't know. I don't think I'd have a chance of getting through Indian Territory by myself. And even if I did, I wouldn't know whichaway to go from there. I'm also thinking I could just forget it. Go on back home."

"Back to Iowa?"

"Yeah. Maybe. I'm also thinking, I could start my own life. But then I'd be a deserter. 'Course, the army probably thinks I'm dead anyhow, or at least in prison. I'm pretty sure they ain't looking for me."

He paused for a moment before continuing.

"I don't know what to do about Old Harm," he said. "Dhu still wants to go after him."

"And you don't?"

"I don't know, Mary Beth." Ben kicked a stone. His hands were shoved deep in his pockets. He stared off across the rolling prairie.

"It looks like it just goes on forever out there," he said.

"It doesn't," said Mary Beth. "After a while there's hill country, and after that there's the ocean."

"I ain't never seen the ocean," Ben said.

"Would you like to?"

"Yeah. I would."

"I've never seen it either," she said. "I just know it's there. I'd like to see it, too — with you."

Ben turned to look at Mary Beth just as she stepped up close to him. He reached out and put his hands gently on her shoulders, and he bent forward and kissed her on the lips, briefly, softly. Then he backed away.

"I'm sorry," he said. "I guess I hadn't ought to done that. I got no right."

"It's okay," Mary Beth said. "Don't be sorry. I liked it."

"All right," he said, with an embarrassed chuckle. "I ain't sorry, then. I'm glad I done it. I liked it, too."

He kissed her again. The kiss was still gentle, still innocent, but this time he held it a little longer. "Mary Beth," he said, "I —"

"What, Ben?"

"I don't know."

"Ben, do you think you might stay here? Not go back to Iowa or back to the war?"

"I would if you'd marry me," he said. "I'd sure stay here."

It had come out so quickly that he could scarcely believe he had said it. He felt his face flush and his heartbeat increase. It was a feeling like fear. He had felt fear before, and he was surprised that this new feeling was so much like it.

"I will, Ben," she said.

* * *

Early called a halt and ordered his troops to dismount. The sergeant gathered them around their captain. Early, in his new black suit, faced his men.

"Gentlemen," he said, "I'm about to make what may be a startling proposition to some of you. I don't know how patriotic any of you are. But it seems to me that we are fighting this war for a handful of rich men, rich plantation owners. We fight and die so that they can retain their wealth and position. Do any of you own plantations and slaves?"

He paused and glanced over the faces of his men. No one answered him.

"I thought not," he said. "Now I ask you, is it right and just and proper that some of us fight and bleed and maybe die in order that the rich remain rich and the poor remain poor? I think not.

"I have never told you exactly what our mission was. I have confided only in Sergeant Crocker. You may have guessed it for yourselves, though. The truth is we were sent to bring a gold shipment up from Mexico. And that is what we have in this wagon."

Early stepped over to the wagon and ripped the canvas cover away, revealing stacks of gleaming gold bars.

"It was bound for the treasury of the Confederacy," he said, "but now I'm thinking along different lines. We now possess the gold; therefore, the gold is ours, if we choose to make it ours. And I so choose. One other thing you may not know is that I killed two men back in that jerkwater town we just left. I killed them to protect our secret. No one knows of this gold but us. You are now free to choose: you may leave this company and go back to the army, or you may stay with me and share equally in the spoils. Make your choice. From this point on there will be no turning back."

"Excuse me, sir," said one of the privates.

"What is it, Sims?"

"What's your plan, sir?"

"First of all to get out of Texas. Then to find a safe spot to rest and make further decisions. We'll divide the gold, as I said, equally. When we've made the division, each man can go his own way with his share."

"I'm with you all the way, Captain," said Sergeant Crocker.

"Me, too," said Sims.

"What about the rest of you?" Early asked.

One private stepped forward. "I'm sorry, sir," he said. "I don't like it. It sounds to me like we'd be outlaws."

"Your opinion is as valid as mine or anyone else's," said Early. "You're free to go. Take your horse and saddle, your guns, and a share of the food and water. As you know, we have no money. Godspeed, Private Connors."

Connors looked around at the men who had been his comrades in arms for so long. He walked over to his horse and mounted up.

"Well," he said, "so long, boys. Captain, sir, I'm sorry. I just —"

"It's all right, Connors," said Early. "You've nothing to apologize for. Go your way, now."

"Good-bye, sir."

Connors turned the horse and started to ride across the open prairie. Early watched him in silence for a moment, then nodded to Crocker. Crocker silently acknowledged the nod, laid his rifle across the shining load in the back of the wagon, took careful aim, and squeezed off a round.

In the distance, Connors threw both arms up in the air and fell off his horse. The horse kept going. Connors lay still.

"Now then," said Early. "Back to business. As I told you before, I killed two men back there. I don't think it's anything to worry about. I saw nothing but old men in that town. But just in case they try to follow us with a posse, I want one man to ride back and scout our trail."

"Turner," said Crocker. "Check it out."

Turner mounted up and rode back toward the town.

Early climbed astride his black stallion. "Let's get going," he said. "The sooner we're out of Texas, the safer we'll be. We'll move along at a leisurely pace until Mr. Turner gets back."

One man climbed onto the wagon seat, and the rest mounted their horses. The former Confederate patrol once again moved toward the Red River.

Almost an hour later Turner, riding hard, came back to rejoin the group. He rode up beside Early, reining his mount down to a walk. "There's a posse coming, sure enough, sir," he said.

"How many?"

"Seven."

"Damn," said Early. "Let's get to the river."

16

Ben and Mary Beth saw Dhu coming down the lane. They figured he had probably witnessed the last kiss, and they were embarrassed. They stepped apart and tried to appear nonchalant, casual, decorous.

Mary Beth assumed that Dhu had come looking for Ben, wanting to talk in private. She politely excused herself and started walking back toward the house.

Dhu tipped his hat as he passed her by, then strolled casually up to Ben. "Well," he said, "have you thought it over?"

"I been thinking," said Ben.

"Yeah, I saw what you were thinking about."

Ben's face heated up, but he didn't respond.

"Are you with me or not?" said Dhu.

"I don't know. The odds are awful bad. It ain't the way you said it was going to be. Your friends aren't coming."

"Hell," Dhu said, turning his back on Ben, "we have a chance to even things with a sadistic son of a bitch who treated us like dogs, and we have a chance at a fortune in gold, but if you'd rather spend your time trying to get a little farm girl in the sack —"

He didn't finish what he was going to say. Ben grabbed him by a shoulder, spun him around, and swung a right into Dhu's jaw. Dhu saw it coming — not in time to duck but in time to roll a little with the punch. Still, it stunned him. He stepped back and shook his head to clear it. Then he took the revolver out of his belt and laid it at the base of a tree a safe distance away.

"I don't want to be tempted," he said. "Well, let's get it on. This has been a long time coming, farm boy."

Ben pulled out his revolver and tossed it aside. He faced Dhu and put up his fists. "Come on," he said.

They moved in and began circling each other tentatively, reaching out now and then with harmless exploratory jabs. Then Ben swung a roundhouse right. Dhu got his left up to partially ward off the blow, but it still hurt. He responded with a right that split Ben's lip, and the Iowan tasted blood. The two of them rushed together in a clinch and grappled. Dhu finally got a leg around behind Ben and tripped him, falling heavily on top of him. Ben's fists pounded Dhu's back and ribs while Dhu struggled to get his arms out from under

Ben's back. When he managed to pull them free, he sat up, and Ben struck him a glancing blow to the chin. Dhu threw a left that caught Ben's ear, making it ring. Suddenly Ben swung a leg up and wrapped it around Dhu's head, throwing him over backwards. Before Dhu could roll away, Ben had his head clamped securely in a leg scissors.

"Ahh," Dhu growled. He rolled one way and then the other, trying to twist himself loose, but Ben's legs were tightly clamped around his head. He put his hands on one leg and pushed. The legs were like a vise. He turned his head until his face was smothered by a thigh, and then he opened his mouth and bit.

Ben screamed in pain and surprise and jerked his legs loose. He scrambled to his feet and limped back a few steps.

Dhu was on his feet in an instant. "Come on, farm boy," he said. "Come on."

"You bit me," Ben said accusingly.

"A fight's a fight, farm boy. No rules. Just fight. Come on."

"I'll pound your face in, you half-breed." Ben swung a low right that dug into Dhu's ribs.

Dhu stepped to his right and gave Ben a hard backhand slap with his left.

* * *

Sam Ed was wandering aimlessly out of the house and down the lane when he heard the clamor from the fight. He ran toward the noise and saw Dhu knock Ben sprawling into the dirt. He turned and ran back to the house, bursting through the door.

"They're fighting out there," he shouted. "Ben and Dhu. They're fighting!"

The rest of the household followed Sam Ed back to the fight. Ben knocked Dhu down just as they arrived. Mary Beth ran between them and put her hands against Ben's chest to hold him back. McClellan got Dhu by the shoulders and pulled him to his feet.

"What's this all about?" he said.

Dhu didn't answer.

"Ben," said Mary Beth, "why are you fighting?"

Ben looked at her. Then he looked away. He thought about what Dhu had said, and he knew that he couldn't tell her.

"It seems to me," said McClellan, "that we'll all have enough fighting to do when them rebels gets here, and that'll be soon enough."

Ben looked over at McClellan. "You still going to fight Old Harm?" he asked.

"Even without the Pins?"
"Yeah," said the old man. "Me and Sam Ed."
Ben stepped unsteadily toward Dhu. "Why didn't you tell me that?" he said.
"Would it have made a difference?"
"Yeah," said Ben. "Yeah, it would."
"Does that mean you're in?"
"Yeah," Ben said, his voice angry, "it does."
"All right." Dhu turned and staggered down the lane toward the house.

Colbert was sitting in front of his tent on a three-legged stool, smoking a corncob pipe, when he saw Dhu ride up on the other side of the river. He stood up and waved. Dhu waved his hat from the opposite bank.
"Are they a-coming?" Colbert shouted.
"They're coming."
Colbert walked down to his ferry and fixed a rope to a tree stump. He tied the other end to the raft as he stepped aboard. Then he pulled on the ropes that ran through pulleys on either side of the river, ferrying himself across to the Texas side.
"They getting close?" he said.
"Pretty close," said Dhu. "They could get here sometime today, or they might

wait until morning. It's hard to tell."

"All right," Colbert said. "Cut her loose, then."

Dhu pulled a knife out of his belt and held it to the rope where it ran through the pulley. "Right here?" he said.

Colbert nodded, and Dhu cut the rope. The raft drifted until it ran to the end of the rope Colbert had used to tie it to the stump on the other side. Then it began to swing toward the north bank. Colbert waved again at Dhu.

The raft continued to swing toward the Indian Territory side of the river. Finally it struck the bank and came to rest. Colbert stepped ashore and studied the scene for a moment. He walked to his tent where he picked up a long coil of rope. He went back to the raft, stepped on board, tied the rope securely to the railing on the far side. Then he threw the other end of the rope over a high tree branch. Stepping back ashore, he began to pull on the end of the rope. The raft was too heavy. He tied it off and walked back to his camp to get one of the horses that had been left there. He led the horse to where the raft waited and tied the rope around the horse's neck. He backed the horse away from the river, slowly drawing the raft up on its edge.

With his ferry thus obviously disabled, Colbert untied the rope, pulled it down from the tree, recoiled it and led the horse back to the camp. He was ready for Old Harm.

Dhu rode back to the McClellan farm. As he rode into the yard, Ben and McClellan came out the front door of the house.

"Get your weapons and mount up," Dhu said. "They're coming."

"Come on, Sam Ed," McClellan shouted.

Herd and his son mounted their horses and followed Dhu down the lane and out onto the prairie. They rode over their new trail to the ford, and Herd and Sam disappeared into the blinds that they had prepared.

Dhu and Ben forded the river. They hid their horses far back in the woods, then found their own hiding places, and settled down to wait. On the Texas side, the two McClellans also waited.

At the river's edge, with Crocker beside him, Early held up his hand to call a halt.

There was no ferry. The line, still tied on the other side of the river, trailed in the water. Some distance away, the raft itself was upended. Across the river, Colbert's tent still stood, with the framework behind it for a new house. The troopers pulled up behind Crocker and Early.

"Mr. Colbert!" Early shouted. "Colbert, are you there?"

Colbert came out from behind the tent. "I'm here," he said.

"We need to cross the river," shouted Early.

"Not here, you ain't," said Colbert. "You can see that for yourself, can't you?"

"Well, damn it, man," said Early, "can you fix it?"

"If I had enough help," said Colbert. "I might get her running again in about a week. Might."

"How the hell can we cross?"

"Few miles east of here, there's supposed to be a ford. I ain't seen it myself, but I hear they're crossing down there."

"How will I find it?"

"Folks have beat a new path to the ford already," said Colbert. "Just follow the tracks."

"Captain," said Crocker, "I did see a fresh trail going east across the grass, back about a mile."

"Get that wagon turned around," said Early. "Hurry it up."

* * *

In his blind by the river crossing, Dhu sat waiting. His bruised face still stung in places. He could also feel a sore spot on his ribs on the right side. But these things didn't matter. Old Harm was coming. He had waited for this moment, planned for it, and it was nearly upon him. He had checked his weapons several times, readying his ammunition for quick reloading. He was worried about the others — not that they might be injured or even killed, but whether or not they would do their jobs right. He was consumed with a hot desire to kill Gordon Early, a feeling he didn't like. He was anxious to have it over and done with. It would be — soon.

Across a trail that was not much more than a path, on the same side of the river, Ben hid in the woods. His thoughts were less clearly focused than Dhu's. He nervously anticipated the arrival of Old Harm and his troops, but he also thought of Mary Beth. He imagined the life he could have with her. He did not want to die, either for revenge or for gold. He would not even have agreed to participate in the ambush had it not been for the fact that Herd McClellan was there with his son. They were to be his new family, and he couldn't let them down. He couldn't see them across the river, though he knew they were there. He prayed for their safety and for his own.

The road to the ferry was narrow, and it took some doing to turn the heavy wagon and the four horses that pulled it. Old Harm shouted orders and curses while the troopers shouted at the horses and one another. Finally the job was done.

Across the river Colbert chuckled until the eight men rode south out of his sight. Then he went back inside his tent.

Early and Crocker wound up behind the wagon after it had been turned around, and they rode in the dust of the others until they had cleared the woods. Then Early spurred his black and raced around the party until he was in the lead again. Crocker followed him. They rode south for a while, until Crocker spotted the fresh wagon tracks in the grass. He pointed off to the east.

"There, Captain," he shouted.

Early and Crocker turned onto the new trail, and the others followed. But just as the last man turned off the road, Early saw a group of riders coming. He called a quick halt.

Surprised, Crocker looked south on the road. He saw them, too. "It's the posse," he said.

Early hated to run, but he also hated to let the gold out of his sight. He had to make a tough decision. Sergeant Crocker was the only man he could trust. He looked over his troopers, and he looked again at the posse, judging how fast they would catch up with him.

"Sergeant," he said, "take two men and get the gold across the river. The rest of the troopers will stay here with me and hold off this posse. We'll catch up with you later."

"Yes, sir." Crocker pointed to the wagon driver and to one other man. "Come on," he said. The wagon raced on toward the ford with two men riding beside it.

Early turned the rest of his men to face the oncoming posse. "We're outnumbered, men," he shouted, "but you're the best of the South. Let's take them head on!"

17

Harvey Eubanks saw the wagon and two horsemen head into the woods, and he saw five other riders turn to face him and his posse. He held up his hand and reined in his mount, but Little Joe either did not see the gesture or chose not to obey it. Across the field, five renegade Confederate soldiers had let out rebel yells and charged directly at the posse. Little Joe reacted to that charge by racing ahead to meet them. All five rebels fired, and Little Joe seemed to fly backwards out of his saddle. His confused horse veered west and kept running. The five renegades kept riding straight for the posse.

The remaining posse members fidgeted nervously behind Eubanks. The old lawman pulled out his rifle and climbed painfully down out of his saddle.

"Dismount," he said to the others. "If you've got a rifle, bring it to play." He turned his horse sideways and stood behind it for a shield. Then he placed his rifle across the saddle and took careful aim. "Do as I do," he said.

The others got down off their horses and

tried to imitate the actions of Eubanks.

The outlaw gang was getting closer. Eubanks squeezed his trigger, and a loud, angry scream escaped from the wide open mouth of Gordon Early as the lawman's lead ball tore through his chest. Old Harm rocked back in his saddle, then leaned forward again, as the big black stallion continued to race ahead. Other posse members fired, and two outlaws fell from their horses' backs. Old Harm was still riding, but his lifeless body had fallen limply across the neck of the stallion.

The two unharmed outlaws reined in their mounts and looked at each other, confused. Ahead of them the black stallion continued to charge the enemy, and finally the lifeless body slipped from its back and fell to the ground, tumbling grotesquely. The horse continued to charge. The two remaining outlaws turned their horses east and hurried after their comrades with the gold wagon.

"Mount up," said Eubanks. "Let's get after them."

Dhu heard the wagon coming and braced himself for action. For a tense moment he waited, and then the wagon rolled into sight on the far side of the river. It was drawn by four horses, and it was obviously carrying a heavy load. Ben had been right. One man was driving the wagon, and Dhu could see two other men riding alongside. He readied himself to fire. Where was Early? Dhu wanted his first shot to find Old Harm. Then he realized something was wrong: he saw only three men where there should have been nine, including Old Harm. Then, from off in the distance on the Texas side of the river, he heard gunshots. Something had gone wrong.

Suddenly it didn't seem right to slaughter these three men with no warning. He stood up to show himself just as the wagon reached the middle of the crossing. "Hold it right there," he said. "You're surrounded."

Crocker pulled out his revolver and fired at Dhu. Dhu dropped down out of sight, but Ben fired from his cover. His bullet hit Crocker in the side of the face. Immediately more shots came from the Texas side of the river, and the other two soldiers dropped into the reddish waters. Dhu jumped up and ran for his horse, shouting to Ben as he ran. "Take care of things here. I'm going to find out what happened back there." He splashed across the river on his horse and headed for the prairie to the south.

Ben left his blind and walked down to the water's edge. He was looking at the bodies floating around the wagon when McClellan and Sam Ed appeared on the Texas side.

"Sam Ed," said McClellan, "can you drive that team?"

"Yes, sir," said Sam Ed. "I ain't seen the team I can't drive."

"Then get it home and inside the barn as fast as you can. I'll come along behind you directly and wipe out the tracks if need be."

Sam Ed waded into the river and made his way out to the wagon. He bumped into the body of the former driver as he climbed up onto the seat, and for an instant he stared at it floating there. He tore his eyes away from the morbid sight and picked up the reins. By yelling at the horses and lashing at them with the reins, he got the wagon turned around and out of the river again, heading for home. By then Ben had mounted up and ridden about halfway across toward Texas.

"Ben," said McClellan, "I'll drag the bodies out if you'll catch all the horses."

"Yeah," said Ben. "I'll do that."

Dhu rode out from under the trees and

onto the open prairie just as the two remaining outlaws were approaching. They were riding hard, and he knew they must be part of the rebel band. He held up his revolver for them to see. "Pull up," he shouted.

One of them fired a shot that tore through the flesh in Dhu's upper arm.

"Damn," he said, and he fired back. The outlaw's horse stumbled, throwing its rider forward. The man rolled in the dirt while Dhu dismounted and the other outlaw continued to charge. Dhu dropped to one knee and took aim. The outlaw fired a wild shot from horseback. Dhu squeezed the trigger and the outlaw tumbled out of the saddle. Dhu quickly cocked his revolver and turned. The outlaw in the dirt had scrambled to his feet, gun in hand. Dhu fired, and the outlaw dropped his gun. He put both hands to his stomach and looked down, stood reeling for a moment, then fell forward.

Dhu climbed back on his horse. Old Harm and four others were still out there somewhere. He rode the trail back toward the Texas Road, and soon he met the posse.

He slowed his pace and rode up to them easy. Harvey Eubanks, on foot, stepped forward to meet him. Dhu saw the badge. He tried to think of something to say to the lawman. He had just killed some rebel soldiers in Texas, a Confederate state. How was he going to explain himself? He didn't want to kill the lawman, but he sure as hell didn't want to go to jail — or to hang. As it turned out, Eubanks saved the situation for him.

"Howdy," said the lawman. "Were those your shots I heard?"

"They were," Dhu said. "Me and some friends."

"You stop the rest of this gang?"

"We got all of them that came this way." Then, thinking quickly, Dhu added, "All except one man who was driving a wagon. He got on across into Indian Territory."

"Well," said Eubanks, "we can't chase him up there. I guess that one's just got off scot-free."

"What about the others?" Dhu said. "The ones who didn't come down our way?"

Eubanks swept his arm out over the prairie.

Dhu followed it with his eyes and saw five bodies where there should have been six. "That all of them?" he asked.

"We found one a few miles back,"

Eubanks said. "I guess the outlaws killed him themselves."

Dhu rode slowly toward the bodies. He passed one, then another. One lay farther back, nearer the trees that lined the river. He turned and rode toward it, his heart pounding in his chest. He could see that the body was dressed in a black suit. He rode on up close and looked down at the twisted figure there before him. It was Old Harm. He was dead, and Dhu felt a sense of relief sweep over him. But there was something else. Looking down at the pathetic, twisted thing that had once contained a human life, he wondered how he could have centered his whole life on that. Old Harm had suddenly become very insignificant.

Eubanks rode up beside him. "You've been hit, son," he said.

"Yeah." Dhu glanced at his arm.

"You better let me see what I can do for it."

"No, thanks," said Dhu. "My friends aren't far. I'll ride on back now. They'll take care of it."

"I've got to gather up all these bodies," Eubanks said. "Where'll I find the others?"

"Just follow these wagon tracks to the river," said Dhu. "You'll find them." As he turned his horse to ride to the McClellan farm, he noticed that the arm was starting to hurt.

Eubanks yelled at him from behind. "What if I've got questions for you and your friends?" he said.

Dhu yelled back over his shoulder, "About halfway between here and the ford there's a lane going into the trees. It leads to Herd McClellan's farmhouse. We'll be there."

Maude was bandaging Dhu's arm, and Mary Beth was pouring coffee for everyone.

"It's all over," Dhu said. "There was a posse behind them. Some of the rebels stopped to try to hold off the posse. We got the rest."

"How'd the posse do?" asked McClellan.

"Wiped them out," said Dhu.

"Old Harm?" said Ben.

"The posse got him. I saw his body."

There was silence for a moment, and then Mary Beth placed a cup of hot coffee on the table in front of Dhu.

"Herd," said Dhu, "where's the wagon?"

"It's in the barn," said McClellan, "hid pretty good."

"That posse might come around to ask

some questions," said Dhu. "I told them the wagon got away from us, across the river."

"They'll never know no different," said McClellan.

"Dhu?" said Ben.

"Yeah?"

"What was a Texas posse doing fighting Old Harm and his boys?"

"I don't know, Ben, but if that sheriff comes in here to talk, be real careful what you say. Let him do the talking."

The posse did show up and Eubanks did ask questions, but Dhu and the others answered them all to the lawman's satisfaction. Actually, Eubanks was so relieved to have gotten all but one of the gang and to have lost only one member of his posse that he was easily satisfied.

Dhu, Ben, and the McClellans were surprised and relieved to learn that Early and his men had turned outlaw. That had gotten them off the hook with the sheriff and had brought in the posse to help clean out the rebels.

Maude served coffee, and Eubanks and his posse said their thanks and their farewells and headed back home. Maude and Mary Beth prepared supper. It was eaten in near silence. The cool late evening settled in, and Dhu went outside and sat on the porch. Ben and Mary Beth were walking down the lane. McClellan came out on the porch with his pipe. Dhu was staring off into the darkness.

"It was all so pointless after all," said Dhu. "I never even saw Old Harm until he was already dead."

"What?" said McClellan. "Pointless? Hell, boy, I'm going to have the biggest damn horse ranch in all of north Texas. That ain't pointless."

Down the lane Dhu saw Ben and Mary Beth returning. He leaned back against the corner post on the porch. His arm was throbbing.

McClellan turned toward Ben. "What do you say, son?" he said. "Is it pointless to have the biggest damn horse ranch in north Texas?"

"No, sir," said Ben. "I'd say there was a whole lot of point to that."

"You see?" McClellan said to Dhu. "Ben understands."

"I understand you, Herd," said Dhu. "It's just me that I'm having trouble with."

"Now I don't understand you," McClellan said.

Ben stepped forward and studied Dhu's

face there in the dim light. "What is it, Dhu?" he said.

"It's just that ever since we broke loose from those rebs, I've had one thing on my mind," said Dhu. "*Get Old Harm.* That's all I could think about. Down there at the river, I wasn't worried about whether or not any of you might get shot. I was worried about whether or not we'd get Old Harm. That's all. And before that, Ben, I said something to you that I shouldn't have said. I didn't mean it. That's why you hit me, and you had a right. I was wrong, but I was eaten up with wanting to get Old Harm."

"Well," said Ben, "what you said wasn't all right, but we can just forget it, can't we? I got mad, too, and I said something I shouldn't have. I called you a name. I called you —"

"I know what you called me," Dhu said. "Forget it."

"I just want you to know I'm sorry I said it."

"All right. Forget it."

For a moment no one spoke. Dhu continued to stare out into the darkness, and Ben stared at the ground. Mary Beth stood off to one side, and McClellan stood on the porch puffing his pipe.

"What are you going to do?" said Ben.

Dhu looked up suddenly, as if startled out of a reverie. "Me?" he said.

"Yeah," said Ben. "You. What are you going to do?"

"I don't know. I have to go help old Colbert put his ferry back in working order. I promised him I'd do that."

"You ain't going to be much help with that arm," said McClellan. "We'll all go. We'll get the job done faster that way anyhow. Least we can do for the man."

"Good," said Dhu. "Thanks."

"After that?" said Ben.

Dhu didn't answer.

Ben walked over to Mary Beth and put an arm around her shoulders. "I'm staying here," he said. "Me and Mary Beth, we're going to get hitched. And I'm staying here to help Herd build up this place. We're going to build it up into the biggest damn horse ranch in north Texas."

Dhu smiled. "I'm glad for you," he said. "But, say, Herd, is Ben the best you can do for a son-in-law?"

"Well," McClellan said, scratching the stubble on his chin, "with our new station in life, I wouldn't want Mary Beth to marry beneath her, you know, and Ben here is the richest young man I know, except for you, that is, and you never asked."

"Papa," said Mary Beth.

"You never did answer my question, Dhu," said Ben.

"No. I guess not."

"Why don't you stay here?"

"I second that," said McClellan. "It's going to be a big ranch. And we'll need some good help."

Dhu stood up and walked a few steps out into the darkness. He inhaled the clean, fresh air deep into his lungs. Old Harm was dead, and all the feelings of hatred and rage and resentment were gone with him. Back home in the Cherokee Nation there was nothing left for Dhu. If he left Ben and the McClellans now, where would he go? He turned back toward Ben.

"I really wish you'd stay," said Ben.

Dhu walked back up onto the porch and stood by Herd McClellan.

"Well," he said, "I just might stick around for a while. I'm not sure this Iowa farm boy knows much about horses anyhow — unless they're plow horses."

"He'll learn," said McClellan. "He'll learn real fast."

About the Author

ROBERT J. CONLEY, a member of the Cherokee tribe, was born in Gushing, Oklahoma, in 1940. He has taught Indian Studies and English at colleges around the country, most recently at Morningside College in Sioux City, Iowa, and was an assistant programs manager with the government of the Cherokee Nation in Oklahoma. He is the author of eight previous novels and a collection of short fiction, *The Witch of Goingsnake and Other Stories*, which includes "Yellow Bird: An Imaginary Autobiography," the winner of the 1988 Spur Award for Best Short Story from the Western Writers of America. Conley currently lives and writes in Tahlequah, Oklahoma (the capital city of the Cherokee Nation), with his wife Evelyn, who is also Cherokee.